## About the Author

Joan Brodie is a young woman from the midwest who always had a knack for eroticism and adult fiction. She refuses to confine herself to the walls of modesty and chooses to be bold and loud with her writing in hopes of envoking real pleasure in her readers. She enjoys anime, psychological thrillers, and crime fiction aside from Eroticism. Her personal life philosophy is to think as if there is no box to think outside of.

# Without Warning

# Joan Brodie

# Without Warning

Olympia Publishers
*London*

www.olympiapublishers.com
OLYMPIA PAPERBACK EDITION

Copyright © Joan Brodie 2024

The right of Joan Brodie to be identified as author of
this work has been asserted in accordance with sections 77 and 78 of
the Copyright, Designs and Patents Act 1988.

All Rights Reserved

No reproduction, copy or transmission of this publication
may be made without written permission.
No paragraph of this publication may be reproduced,
copied or transmitted save with the written permission of the publisher,
or in accordance with the provisions
of the Copyright Act 1956 (as amended).

Any person who commits any unauthorised act in relation to
this publication may be liable to criminal
prosecution and civil claims for damage.

A CIP catalogue record for this title is
available from the British Library.

ISBN: 978-1-80439-347-5

This is a work of fiction.
Names, characters, places and incidents originate from the writer's
imagination. Any resemblance to actual persons, living or dead, is
purely coincidental.

First Published in 2024

Olympia Publishers
Tallis House
2 Tallis Street
London
EC4Y 0AB

Printed in Great Britain

# Acknowledgements

Thank you to my dear Serena for being my muse. To Carlia, for being my voice of reason and to Jamie, for being my first fan.

# Chapter 1

I remember the first time I told anyone about my sexuality. It was sometime during my senior year at Douglas High. I stood across from Shayna, a friend of mine. I stared into her eyes with my heart pounding in my chest and thought over and over about how to get the words out of my head. My mouth was dry. My stomach twisted and churned. Girls and boys from various classrooms flooded the halls pushing and shoving their way to the exits. I was ready to leave school too, but I was in no rush to go home. I thought over and over about what to tell her and how to let the words out.

"Spit it out, Azlyn. You can tell me anything," she offered her reassurance.

I sighed, took a deep breath and let the words out. "I like women... I mean I like boys too. I just I don't know."

"Okay, I like girls and boys too. What are you getting at?"

I bit my lip and sighed. "No, Shayna, that's not what I meant... I mean... I mean... I'm bisexual."

She blinked a few times and stared back at me doe eyed. Then a grin spread across her face.

"No way. Azlyn, that's not fair. I don't believe you."

I frowned. She was laughing. I suppose this was better than her being horrified and running away well maybe it wasn't too late for that.

"I'm not kidding," I mumbled with tears pricking at the corner of my eyes. Would I lose my closest friend over this? What did she think of me? Thoughts ran in loops around my mind, and I struggled to keep my breathing calm.

"Azlyn... you don't have anything to worry about."

She put a hand on my shoulder and pulled me in for a hug. She kissed my cheek and I held her back and sighed. Shayna had a pure heart. I shouldn't have doubted her.

Afterwards we walked hand in hand towards the exit. She told me about a party she wanted me to come with her to after school. I knew my parents would freak if they found out so I told her I would go check it out, but I wouldn't stay long. She told me that her older sister was going to be in the area, and I could call her to take me home when I was ready to leave.

Sometime after my parents fell asleep, I snuck out the window and walked down the street to her sister's car. Shayna was in the back and excited to see me. I didn't know the host of the party, so Shayna told me a little about her, how they were close and hung out sometimes. She told me she would introduce me to her but shortly after we arrived at the party, Shayna found some other friends to run off with. I didn't mind. I was happy just to get a break from being home. My parents weren't the most understanding type of people. They were very old fashioned in their discipline and their attitudes. Things weren't that great for me, a closeted bisexual, at home.

I remember Shayna joining a large group of friends off to the side and seeming to enjoy herself. I didn't like big groups, so I lurked around in the corner by the beer someone snuck in. Eventually I found some of my other friends and spent the rest of the night talking and dancing with them. I remember sneaking back inside a little after midnight and scrubbing my teeth with my fingers to get rid of the beer smell. Those were times I cherished. The private life I led in the shadows.

Oddly enough, after high school I ended up attending a Catholic College. Solely because they were the first school that accepted me, and they were located a few hours away from home. Safe enough to say my parents wouldn't be visiting. My first few years went by in a blur. I made new friends, went to parties, did well in my classes. I was an average student, and I didn't stick out much. I didn't put in the effort to either.

When senior year came, we got to choose our own apartments instead of the regular college dorms. The apartments were co-ed and a little ways off campus. I had learned already that the college boys were just as immature and gross as the high school ones, so I opted for a female roommate. I fared well with previous roommates so I figured things would go just as smooth with this one. When we got our roommate packets in the mail with their photo and contact information, I shot her a text introducing myself and letting her know I was already in the room. I didn't get a reply, but I didn't think much of it.

I arrived at the apartment shortly after noon and spent most of my time unpacking and setting up the room. The rooms were medium sized. There was a few sofas and chair in the living room and a small countertop with bar chairs in the kitchen. It wasn't bad in my opinion. I was busy sorting through my boxes for my textbooks when I heard a knock on my door. The door was open, and I thought I was alone, so I was alarmed when I realized someone had come in, but I looked up quickly and realized it was just my roommate. Rebecca Hall.

"Hey."

"Hey, I'm Azlyn."

"I know."

She paused for a moment, so I took the fake smile off my face and went back to unpacking. I wasn't necessarily dissatisfied with her or anything, but I got the impression she wasn't that thrilled to have a roommate. I shrugged it off. Maybe I was reading too deep into things. When night came, I had finished packing and my room was set up. I started reading some of the course material I had due for the first day of second semester tomorrow. I heard her fumbling around in the kitchen and finally going into the living room to watch some reality show. I knew she was in the Nursing Program, so I figured maybe she didn't have any reading work due like I did. After I finished my assignment, I was scrolling through my phone looking through everyone's move-in day selfies on social media when she came to my doorway again.

"Hey, want to watch this show with me?"

I bit my lip and thought for a moment. I finally decided that maybe this could be a great chance for us to warm up to each other, so I joined her. The show was some meet the bride type shit, so I mindlessly watched it with her. I let my mind roam elsewhere while she chatted away about what was happening in the show. She seemed excited about it like it was the greatest thing in the world. I preferred crime thrillers and drama. When she tapped my shoulder and asked me to look at her favorite part of the show, I glanced at the TV then glanced back at her. It was my first time getting to look at her outside of the roommate brochure.

She had long legs and creamy light brown skin. It looked like she moisturized and exfoliated on a regular basis. I wanted to touch her. Just out of curiosity of course. But I kept my hands to myself. I let my eyes roam over her body and explore her plump cleavage poking through the top of her tank top. I started thinking about her pink lips and pale hazel eyes. She was attractive. I figured she was straight judging by the sharp edges on her painted fingernails and the picture of a boy on her lock screen that lit up with each notification from an Adam. I turned my attention back towards the TV and repositioned my legs. I felt a sudden warmth between my legs and an urge to touch myself.

"Hey, um, I have an early class so I'm going to head to bed, okay?"

"Oh, okay."

When I was back in my room, I quickly closed the door behind me. I slipped out of my shorts, and tank top and crawled under my soft cotton comforter. I swirled my tongue around my fingers and dove them in between the folds of hot slippery flesh that baked beneath my panties. I had begun to soak through my shorts and dampen my panties. I parted the folds and fondled the small hole that my warm juices slipped out of and bit my lip. When I couldn't bear to taunt myself further, I slipped a finger inside and hooked my fingers in deep within my sex. Finger after finger, I pleasured myself. Diving each one in and out of my soaking hole and moaned as each one brushed and stroked against my throbbing walls. I gasped and moaned as ecstasy invaded my chest and circled its way down to my womb.

My pierced nipples hardened and with my free hand I twisted and pulled at each one. My moans grew louder as I weakened under pleasure. I had long forgotten about the presence of my unsuspecting muse that lay meters away on the other side of the wall in a bed of her own. The thought of her listening in and perhaps being inspired to grope and stroke her own self aroused me blissfully. As my orgasm grew to climax, I bit down on my bottom lip trying to stifle my moans as best I could. My clit throbbed and twitched under my relaxed hand. I rolled over onto my left side and tasted my drenched fingers. I decided it would be best not to go to class smelling like sex, so I pulled out a fresh change of panties. When I opened my door, I startled her as she was walking into her room next door. I smiled and headed to the shower. I figured she was ready for bed as well. Little did I know she was standing outside the door and had heard everything.

# Chapter 2

Church bells rang through the walls of Rosewood's English building doing little to drown out the chatty females that sat in the row behind me. All about their extravagant winter adventures and how one girl got gifted a car for Christmas and the other some name brand sweater and jewelry. I thought about my own holidays and how they were a blur just like every other day for me. I had some good gifts over the years but as I got older and picked up some adult weight, my parents found it comical to gift me with clothes that were two sizes too big. I still had to pretend to be grateful; after all, at least I got something right?

The teacher passed around the syllabus and I sat mine on the edge of my desk. When I tried to grab it again to look over it with the class it slipped onto the floor underneath the heel of the woman in front of me. She had smooth caramel skin and wore small black heels. She noticed the paper had slipped so she bent down to pick it up. I tapped her shoulder and she turned around to face me. The curls in her hair bounced and framed her face drawing my attention to her piercing brown eyes.

"Thanks."

She handed me the form and smiled. "I'm Carver."

I nodded and introduced myself back. She turned back around, and I did my best to tune into what the teacher was saying about quizzes and exams. My mind like always was elsewhere. I was dreamer. It was hard for me to sit still. The teacher discussed an end of year project we must do and that we would need to partner up. I looked around as pairs began forming and I didn't know what to do. I didn't know anyone in class, and I didn't particularly like the idea of partner work. I always got stuck with most of it. Carver glanced around and then her eyes fell on me. She smiled and asked if we could partner up.

"Um… yeah that's fine with me."

We went over the worksheet, and it turns out we both were to write an essay on a book of our choice and then give a presentation on it. I absolutely hated writing essays for class, but Carver seemed thrilled with the idea. Her face lit up as she spilled about book ideas. Her excitement was contagious. My mind began to wander with ideas of my own.

After class we decided to meet up for lunch. We started talking about what we each chose to eat. I told her I was meat free, so I had a Mediterranean veggie sandwich. She mentioned how meat was her one true love in life and how she could not live off salads alone. Carver was tall, had long legs, and wide pink lips. When she laughed a strand of brown locs tumbled from the clutch of her ear and mingled with the freckles painted across her smooth light brown skin. Her pink lips spread across her face, pushing her freckles up against her creamy brown eyes that darted from her slender fingers and back to me. I smiled as my mind began to wander into places it shouldn't have dared to venture.

"So, what about you? Where are you from?"

I blinked a few times unclear of when I lost track of the conversation, but we were talking about our origins. I told her that I was from Missouri which was three hours away from here. Far enough away that my parents would not want to drive every weekend and close enough to something I was familiar with. She told me about how she played volleyball and basketball throughout high school and came here on a sports scholarship. I was athletically challenged so I came here after winning a scholarship on an essay I had written. Something about my struggles with being a child adopted by strangers and how I felt like an unwanted guest in a place I struggled to call home. Of course, I didn't use those words exactly but thankfully she got the impression of how I didn't want to talk about that. Nothing from my childhood was worth bridging a bond over. The less I had to recall, retell and remember the better.

Soon the conversation shifted to our music interests; we shared a similar love for grunge and soul music. That was a rare combination I usually never related to people with. Joy spread across my face as I eagerly engaged in the conversation and exchanged song choices with her. This woman began strumming the strings in my heart as she shared songs with me that I had already saved to my playlist. I began to see the bond between us growing stronger and imagined what it would be like when it blossomed.

Later that evening as I sat in the lower lobby of the apartment, I realized I couldn't get my mind off her long enough to focus on the reading that lay before me. I was torn between wanting to focus on it and focus on her. I rubbed my eyes and walked around for a bit, but it was no use. I needed a break. I stepped out of the lobby and went into the bathroom. I splashed water on my face and sighed as I gazed at my sagging expression.

"You sounded like you were up all night."

I swiveled around at the voice behind me and saw Rebecca standing between me and the stalls. Her hands on her hips and a mischievous smirk painting her face.

"What?" I asked startled.

"Oh, you know, the walls are pretty thin. I mean no need to

be embarrassed; we all do it."

She stepped closer to me causing me to press my back against the sink.

"I… "

My heart pounded in my chest pausing my speech. I knew it was possible she could hear, but I didn't think she really did. I couldn't tell if she was proud or disgusted. Knots began to form in the pit of my stomach.

"I… I—"

She moaned mockingly. "That's all I heard all night. If anyone should be tired, it should be me. What are we going to do about this?"

"I'm sorry."

"I'm sorry is not going to cut it. I mean, I can't keep missing my sleep so how about we go and let the school's landlord know we need to change apartments."

"No! No… I'm sorry it won't happen again."

Panic seeped into my chest as my brain raced around trying to find a reasonable solution to this. I couldn't bear the thought of losing my housing and moving back in with my parents.

"With the way you were moaning and groaning? I highly doubt that. Hmm, maybe we can come to an understanding."

She stepped forward and placed her finger on my chest. I couldn't move away any further with my back pressed into the sink.

"How about… you do my homework for English class. I hate deciphering poetry. What nurse needs to do that anyways?"

"For the whole semester? You must be joking. I can't do that."

"Then I guess the landlord needs to know."

She began walking towards the door and I reached out to

grab her wrist to stop her.

"No, please anything else. It's my Senior year. I can't fuck up."

She sighed and twisted her wrist around to grab mine. "Then how about… " She took my hand and placed it on the back of her thigh beneath her black skirt. She pulled it upwards raising her skirt. "Grab it."

I tried shaking my head and she kissed my lips. I couldn't believe this was happening. She moved my hand to the front of her panties and rubbed her flesh against my fingertips. She moaned against my lips and pulled her panties down to stick my hand inside of her soaking wet cunt.

"Fuck me."

Lost in pleasure as warm moisture leaked in the crevices of my fingers, I hooked my fingers around her mound and dove my fingers deep in her hole. She moaned and rode her hips into me, forcing my fingers further inside of her. She bit the side of my neck and stuck her hand up my shirt to grab hold of my right breast.

My fingers entered her faster and she clutched my breast harder. I moaned and bit her bottom lip. Her hips bucked and she dug her nails in my breast. When the kiss broke, she sighed and swore under her breath. She trembled in my grasp as soft, slippery fluid dripped from her hot soaking sex. I gasped and stared back at her as she pushed me away.

"See. I knew we could come to an understanding."

My heartbeat thudded in my ears. I panicked when I heard the toilet flush in another stall. I caught a glimpse of Rebecca snickering as she sped out of the restroom. I hurried and washed my hands and made it out the door just as the stall door opened.

I found it difficult to go back to the apartment knowing

Rebecca might be there. I had no idea how to even face her right now. I closed the front door behind me and glanced around the corner to make sure she wasn't in sight then dashed to my room and shut the door. What the fuck even was that? Was this some sort of sick game? I racked my head for answers but found none. I thought maybe it wouldn't be a bad idea to change roommates. I wouldn't even know what to tell the landlord. It was me after all that fucked her and not the other way around. I couldn't even lie and say I didn't find any pleasure in it. I could still smell her on my fingers. I slipped off my clothes and laid on my bed. I had no idea what the hell I got myself into.

# Chapter 3

It was around 6 pm when I woke up from a nap after finishing my day. From lectures and assignments to the near-death experience of being almost caught in the bathroom with Rebecca my head was starting to pound with endless thoughts flying around. I hadn't seen her all afternoon or heard her come in. I wasn't sure how I was going to face her. I couldn't believe she overheard me and then made me finger her in public. I rolled over and dove my head into my pillows and sighed. I feared bumping into Rebecca but the gnawing in the core of my stomach grew more intense as I lay flat on it now. I decided that eating something could help get my mind back together, so I made my way to the kitchen to scrounge for something to eat.

    As I pulled out the bread and toppings for a PBJ sandwich, I heard Rebecca come in gasping and sighing. When she rounded the corner, I saw her lips locked onto a guy that I presumed was Adam. He grunted and pulled her closer into him. He struggled taking off her bra and she assisted him while they made their way into her bedroom. Just before she closed the door, she gave me a long lust-filled stare. I bit my lip and sighed. I wondered what this was for her. A game? It must be. I suddenly lost my appetite. I grabbed a bottle of left-over vodka and went into the lounge where I had left some schoolwork due the next day for my philosophy and psychology classes. I took a few swigs of the bottle and did my best to concentrate on the text in front of me. I couldn't help but lose focus every other paragraph or so as the moans of Rebecca filled my ears and flashbacks to the restroom blurred my vision. I wanted to tell her to keep it down. I wanted to tell her to stop and fuck me instead. I wanted a lot of things that weren't going to happen. I didn't want to play this sick game of hers. My sexuality wasn't a toy. Part of me knew and accepted that but another part of me that had been sex deprived all winter break craved a different chain of events.

Somehow, I made it through my philosophy reading. I was four shots down and still suffocated by Rebecca's cries. I figured if this was her payback for last night then what the hell was that this morning? I shook my head and started pummeling through my English assignment. Rebecca came out of the room and stretched, revealing herself to my prying eyes. I sighed.

"Can we talk?" I asked.

She swiped the bottle of vodka from me and finished it in a single gulp. "Not really."

She headed back into her room and moments later I heard giggling and then silence.

The silence didn't last long. I soon heard them bickering about something and things were being thrown around. I wondered if I should check on her but thought it would be better to mind my business. Her door slammed and I saw Adam walking away from her as she was hurling curses at him. The front door slammed, and he was gone. She was mumbling something about how he wasn't good enough for her and how she couldn't believe they were still together. I was glad her attention wasn't on me, so I slipped back into my room.

The next day I met up with a friend from another class. We had lunch together and he talked to me about this party that was coming up that he wanted to go to. I figured it being our last semester here there would be a lot of parties happening. I told him I was down to go and got the information about it from him. Drew was tall, dark skinned and had almond shaped deep brown eyes. He had broad shoulders and toned arms and legs. He was on the basketball team and pretty much knew everybody here. He was sociable like that. He paused the conversation to scroll through his social media and I took the opportunity to ask him something.

"Hey, Drew... do you know a girl named Rebecca?"

He thought for a moment and stuck a fry in his mouth before answering. "Yeah, I think that's Adam's girl. Why?"

"Well, she's my roommate."

"Oh damn. Good luck with that. I hear she's bat shit crazy; at least that's what Adam tells us."

He continued with his fry munching and I sat for a moment wondering just how crazy he meant. I suppose I got a glimpse the other day.

"Yeah? I'll try to be careful then."

"Yeah, trust me, that's a tree you don't wanna bark up."

Drew knew about my sexuality and often invited me to parties to help him pull girls. I get that he was trying to warn me not to try anything with her, but I wanted to tell him that that ship had already sailed. I didn't know where this road with her was heading but I had a feeling it wouldn't be good to continue things like this with her. Before I made it back to class, I made it a point to check every stall in the bathroom for any sign of Rebecca.

When I was satisfied with my search, I did my business and headed back to class. On the way there, I bumped into Carver, and we walked into class together. Somehow seeing her eased my mind. We sat next to each other and talked about how our night went. Mine was uneventful and hers was full of work. She told me about this bar she works at to pay for her off campus apartment. She said I was lucky for having the scholarship that covered everything for me. I shrugged it off. I guess I was, but I definitely didn't get that the easy way. The teacher began talking about the objectives for today. Carver cracked jokes in my ear, and we almost got busted a few times for not paying attention. When we were allowed to break out into our own conversations to discuss our project, we were relieved.

"So, what are you majoring in?"

I thought for a moment about what to say. I told her psychology and she asked me what I wanted to do when I grew up and at first, I didn't know what to say. I had thought about it of course but picturing me doing it in my head always felt awkward to me.

"I want to be... a sex therapist."

I let the words ooze out of my mouth slowly and watched for her disgusted reaction but there was none. She nodded her head as if I said something as normal as being a teacher.

"Have you told the department chair?"

"What? No way. They're not going to take me seriously and they'll try to baptize me or something."

She laughed and started writing down some information for our project.

"Seriously, Azlyn, I think that's cool. I mean... to be a sex therapist I assume you'd have to have some experience?"

There was a hidden question in what she asked so I smiled suddenly feeling bashful. I told her that in any profession it's best to have experience. I decided to dance around her question instead of giving a direct answer. She noticed and smirked.

After class I packed up my things and waved bye to Carver as she headed off to go get ready for work. I had my own parttime thing to get to myself. From Friday evening and Saturday evening I worked a few hours at the Mental Health Clinic on campus. I mostly pushed paper, filed case files and made phone calls for Mrs. Valorie, the psychologist there. I made my way straight there instead of heading home to drop my books off. I didn't need to change; our school wore a uniform that was perfectly fine to wear. I straightened my skirt and made my way across campus to the clinic.

# Chapter 4

## Rebecca

I kicked my feet up on the bed and pushed my notebooks aside. I hadn't heard from Adam all day and that concerned me. We got into a fight the other day about how he still wasn't ready to meet my dad. I mean we've been dating for two years. How is he not ready? He feeds me that same bullshit every time. Thinking about it was bringing the anger back. I rolled my eyes and sent him another text telling him to come over. I laid on my back staring up at the ceiling with my phone on my chest waiting patiently impatiently for his text. Minutes felt like hours before it finally vibrated and all he had to say was 'what's up'. I slammed my phone down and left the room in a huff.

I dug through the fridge looking for any leftover wine and didn't find any, so I slammed the door annoyed even more. I turned around and thought for a moment about how I was going to spend my night and then as I was looking around the room, I noticed Azlyn's door was open. I hadn't heard her come in yet so I decided I would go peek around.

Her room was nothing fancy. Black sheets, black curtains, a few pink pillows, and clothes littered all over the floor. I kicked them aside and sat down on her bed. It was comfortable, but it had nothing on my pillow top hybrid mattress. I laid back and closed my eyes. I thought about the way her fingers pulsed inside of me and felt my nipples stiffen and my clit quiver. I had to give it to her. She was good with her hands. But when I remembered why, my irritation rose slightly.

It was senior year at Douglas High, and I had just transferred to Kansas City, Missouri. I didn't have many friends... well, I had plenty but not many real ones. I found truth, love and honesty in the arms of Shayna. She was the only one in the group that adored me for me and didn't think to ask me for money or rides or favors. We just hung out for the sake of being around each other. I wasn't sure when I first discovered my own sexuality. I knew I liked boys growing up because all my friends did, and it is what normal little girls do. Fawn over boys. But something in me woke up when I met Shayna. I wanted to be near her all the time, and I absolutely had to know her whereabouts. As we grew closer the feelings I had for her intensified. I wanted to touch her in places only boys were allowed to. I wanted to hold her, kiss her, consume her. I guess it was a type of love at first sight. But that love was stolen from me.

I'm not sure how much time had passed since I laid in her bed. I ran my hands over the top of my mound and slipped them down between my legs. My fingers traced my skin over my panties causing them to become damp with my juices. I closed my eyes and imagined it was Shayna fucking me earlier and not Azlyn. I imagined her fingers rolling around the hole of my cervix and pushing against my walls. Gentle moans slipped from my mouth and my hips rolled around beneath my touch. I moved my panties aside and pulsed my fingers inside my quivering hole. With my free hand I fondled my nipples that hardened under my touch. I pinched and pulled them imagining Shayna kissing my neck and biting my lip. Soon the pleasure built inside me, and I thrust my fingers faster. I cried out loud begging Shayna to touch me more and pull my nipples harder.

"Ah fuck, Shayna please."

I begged and begged until I couldn't hold back any longer. I gripped the sheets and dove in my pussy harder and harder. Plunging against my cervix with each thrust and pulling at my nipples. With a final cry, I unleashed a wave of pleasure that squirted out and dripped down my trembling legs. I sloshed my fingers around in my juices and wiped my fingers clean on her covers. I laughed to myself thinking about what her face would look like when she noticed or if she even would. I massaged my breast and waited until the euphoria died down before I made my way back to my room. Just as I made my way inside and shut the door, I heard a knock at the door and my phone ping. I ignored the phone and went to the door only to see Adam looking down on me.

"What the hell, you didn't answer your phone?"

I realized I never picked it up when I flung it. I shrugged my shoulders and walked him over to the couch.

"I don't know, I lost it for a sec. I guess."

"Man, whateva'."

"Come on, Adam, don't be like that!"

"Be like what?"

I crossed my arms and stood over him while he sat down on the couch glancing at the TV and back at me.

"Seriously, babe. I don't want to argue right now."

I gave him my best pout but all he did was roll his eyes and start looking around for the remote.

"Come on, I'm serious."

He smacked his lips and looked me up and down.

"Man, whateva', prove it."

He licked his lips and looked down at the bulge in his pants and back up at me. I rolled my eyes and bent down between his legs. He was lucky I was in the mood for this. I unbuckled his pants and his dick launched out in front of me. Adam had a big dick but what was the point when he didn't know how to use it? I got more pleasure from my own fucking fingers. If I wanted to enjoy myself, I had to do things my way. I trailed my tongue up from the base of his dick and slurped on the tip taking it in my mouth. I bopped my head up and down and let his dick knock against the back of my throat as I took each inch deeper than the last. I swirled my tongue around the tip and sucked until it plopped out of my mouth. I knew he loved when I did that. He tossed his head back and let out a few 'fucks'. I figured this should've been more than enough for his sorry ass. I thrust it in the back of my throat, coating it with my saliva. I wanted to get it nice and wet so it would be easy to slip right in me with no extra hassle. My hole was small and tight and taking him in me had always been a challenge unless I put it in myself. Dumb fuck probably barely knew where the hole was. I slurped his dick and plopped it out of my mouth. Finally, it was ready. I slid off my panties and straddled him. I was ready to take him for a ride.

# Chapter 5

Since it was Saturday, I didn't need to wear my school uniform to work. Instead, I opted for a black tank top dress and my black flats. I pulled my hair into a high ponytail and made my way out the door, thankfully without waking up Rebecca.

When I made it to the office, I greeted Mrs. Valorie who was on her cell phone and walking around the office. She smiled at me and motioned for me to come in. I sat down at my usual desk right outside her office and got to work organizing the files on the desk. When she finished her phone call she perched on the edge of my desk.

"You look worn out already and the day has barely started, ma'am."

"Sorry, I stayed up a bit late studying."

"You're fine. How have you been?"

"I've been good. Break was well... break."

She gave me a sympathetic tap on the shoulder.

"How have things been for you, Val?"

"Good. Good."

I could hear a faint 'but' in her voice, but I didn't want to ask about it. I eyed Mrs. Valorie up and down. She had red hair cut into a bob and milky brown skin adorned with shapely legs and plump brown lips. She was a beautiful woman. I admired her. In all respects.

"How are things at home?"

"Come on, Val, you're not going to psych me."

"What? It's just a simple question, Azlyn."

"Not from you it's not. There's always some deep motive."

"Really? And you get that from a question?"

"One of many, ma'am."

I smiled and she chuckled.

"It's good you're back, Azlyn."

"It's nice to see you too."

She grabbed some folders off my desk and handed them to me. She asked me to go through them and file them alphabetically in the back storage room. I got right on it, and she headed into her office. After sorting out the folders I carried them bunch by bunch into the storage room and placed them in their correct drawers. I was trying to open one of the drawers and it wouldn't budge. I tried to put my back into it but that was a bad idea. The folders tucked under my arm slipped out and spread in a small pile on the floor.

"Shit."

I quickly knelt and began picking up the folders and one caught my eye. It had a familiar name labeled across it: Rebecca Hall. I knew these were private folders containing countless tales from students that waltzed into her office but something in me was pleading with my voice of reason. I moved to pick up the folder when I heard movement behind me.

"Something catch your eye?"

I closed my eyes and sighed. Thankfully Val had come in before I made a terrible decision. I picked up the folder and it slid across the tip of my finger and fell to the floor again.

"Fuck, Fuck!"

"Here, let me see."

I showed Val the tiny paper cut on my right index finger. She took a look at my finger and told me about how it would heal soon and wasn't too bad. She sure had a lot to say for someone not currently in pain.

"It hurts."

She looked in my eyes and pulled me a little closer to her with my finger still in her hands. I watched as she brought my finger up to her lips and kissed it. When a drop of blood got on her lips, she licked it off and caressed my wound with her tongue. I opened my mouth to object, but her lips soon found mine and we embraced in a deep kiss. Flashbacks of how we ended things last semester came floating back into the forefront of my mind.

On one drunk holiday I found her slumped at her desk from one too many drinks from the office party a few hours prior. She had been dealing with a divorce threat from her husband. He frequently snooped through her phone and earlier that day he had confronted her with evidence he found of her exchanging flirtatious and provocative texts with another woman. He was furious and threatened that if she didn't "get help" he would divorce her. She sobbed in my arms that night and told me about how much grief it was giving her to have to give up half of who she was for the man she loved. I wondered how anyone could call something so painful love, but she insisted that I was too young to know what she meant. Maybe she was right. One thing I was not too young to know was that if love made me feel that much pain, then maybe I didn't need it. Pain was something I had more than enough of.

As I was comforting her that night, she decided that she would forsake her professionalism, forsake her vows for a moment and all her chains that kept her heart and mind imprisoned she'd unlock. She looked into my eyes, her young protégé, and asked me to close mine. I knew what she wanted and frankly I wasn't dedicated to my own morals enough to resist. When her lips melted against mine, I embraced her willingly.

After we dabbled in the dark arts of taboo with our legs intertwined in one another's we spent some time laughing about the delicious ways she could save her marriage and still embrace her true self. She told me her plans of having a heart to heart, open and honest conversation with him including about the events of tonight. After our unofficial therapy session, we got ourselves redressed and before we could head out, she thanked me for being there for her.

I stood before her now, my tongue locked with hers, wondering if she remembered that night. I broke the kiss and she moved to my neck pulling me against her with her hands gripping my ass.

"Mmm—wait—Val."

She wasn't hearing me, and I only had a few seconds left before my voice of reason was swallowed by ecstasy. Her hands worked their way under my dress and lifted it. She got on her knees and lapped at the damp parts of my panties. By this point I was lost. My willpower was over run, and I wanted her to have her way with me. She pulled my panties aside and trailed her tongue along my pussy lips. She spread the folds of skin with her tongue and slurped at my juices. I braced myself against the wall as her fingers spread my lips and watched her tongue dance across my clit. I gasped and moaned eager to release my juices in her mouth. She slurped and sucked on my clit until I couldn't bear it any longer. I held her head down on my clit and she twirled her tongue round and round and round. My body tensed and convulsed with a release of pleasure.

"Fuck, fuck."

I sighed and she came back up to kiss me. I got on my knees, and she faced the wall and lifted her skirt. She wasn't wearing any panties. I assumed she must've had this planned in her mind from the moment she woke up. I spread her ample cheeks with my hands and lapped at the sticky, sweet juices pouring out of her pussy. I forced my tongue in her hole and licked around and flicked my tongue against her walls. She cried out in ecstasy. I trailed my tongue up to her tail bone and back down to her clit. She tasted clean and sweet. I slurped at her hole and placed a finger inside and pulsed against her walls. She held my hand, forcing it deeper in and out of her trembling hole. I watched as her body tensed and rivers and honey poured down my fingers and dripped onto the floor.

We cleaned ourselves up in the bathroom silently. When we came out she turned towards me and kissed me.

"I missed you."

"How long do you plan to keep this from him?"

I was referring to her husband. The truth was it was hard for her to let this part of her life go. Even before the sex I could tell she wasn't ready.

"I don't know."

She leaned onto the desk and looked off into the distance. I decided I would finish up with the files and head to lunch. I think she needed some time to consider the impact of what just happened. I didn't like being in the middle of her marriage, but she makes it hard for me to resist. I turned towards the glass doors and headed out into the sea of uncertainty.

# Chapter 6

Later that night, I couldn't bring myself to focus on the book we had decided to read for our project. My mind kept circling back to how I left things with Mrs. Valorie. I knew I had a crucial part in this, but I wondered if I was in too deep to back down. I gave my notes a once over and began circling key parts of the book and writing notes to the side about its connection to class. I did my best to take my mind off of Mrs. Valorie. I put her on a shelf in my mind for something to deal with later. I turned my attention once again back to the book.

It focused on how lesbianism has evolved over the years and how women have become empowered with their sexuality. All topics I enjoyed but my mind kept venturing down other lanes. Unable to focus, I decided to put the book down and focus on my other class assignments. Just then, I received a text from Carver. It turned out that she was also struggling to focus and wanted to meet up with me here to discuss about what we've read so far. Disregarding the fact that Rebecca would be home any moment I assured her that it was fine for her to come over. I set up my study materials on the bed so that she would have enough space to work as well. I figured if Rebecca did come home while she was still here, we wouldn't be crowding up the living room or kitchen in case Adam was with her. When she arrived, we poured our best effort into decrypting the text laid out before us: Wild Berries by Q. Sanders.

In the story, Isobel was a character forced by her parents to marry a man and stifle her sexuality. This caused her to act out by falling in love with her nanny and run away with her. They were found by her husband and her family who burned them at the stake and deemed them witches practicing sexual immorality and sin. Carver seemed emotionally invested and decided that we should explore the impact religion has on women's rights to govern their bodies. I decided I would focus on the impact religion has made on female nudity and she explored religion on female sexuality. We wrestled with the pros and cons of presenting this topic to our class knowing that some of them came from backgrounds similar to Isobel and her lover Andrea. But we also strongly believed that the impact of the text could open at least someone's mind to the world around us and the role women play in it.

When our notes were just about complete for the night, we shut our books and I leaned back on the bed trying to sort out the mass of information in my head. I wanted to know what was going through her head. She looked down over her notes and brushed a strand of hair from her face.

"Carver, I—"

"What the hell?"

Just then, Rebecca burst in my bedroom and glared at me. She looked over at Carver who stared back at her with just as much confusion as I had.

"Didn't you hear me calling you?"

"Um, what? No."

I stood up and crossed my arms back defiantly. Who was she to be bursting into my room with no god-damned sense to begin with?

"And who the fuck is this?" She pointed to Carver and sneered at her.

I ignored her question and asked her what the fuck she was doing in my room.

"I can go wherever the fuck I please."

She started walking closer to me and I backed up. Just then Carver stood up with her things packed away. I looked at her and told Rebecca she was a friend. Carver gave me a tight-lipped smile that must've meant this situation was awkward for her.

"Hey, Azlyn, I'm going to head home. It seems like she really needs you."

"Wait no, Carver!"

Carver brushed past Rebecca, and I followed her to the front door ignoring the wall of rage that was Rebecca behind my back.

"Stop for a minute!"

Carver turned to look at me and glanced back at Rebecca.

"I'm sorry, I don't know what her deal is."

"It's fine. I don't want to get between whatever this is."

She motioned towards Rebecca. I turned and looked at her. She leaned against the frame of my door picking at her nails. I looked back at Carver.

"It's nothing."

"I guess. See ya later, girl."

I let Carver out the door and locked it behind her. My mind was swirling with rage and worry.

"What's going on?"

"What's going on? What's going on is you having bitches up in here and ignoring me when I call you!"

"I'm sorry, are you my mother?"

Just then she charged at me and wrapped her hands around my throat. I put my arms up and tried to push her off me but to no avail. She forced her knee between my legs and pressed into me. She stared into my eyes, and I turned away from her. I felt her tongue press against the crease of my shoulder and trail up the side of my neck and draw small circles on my jawbone. I closed my eyes and flashbacks of the bathroom incident came to mind. I didn't know what I wanted in this moment, but I knew I didn't want things to end up like that. With her other hand still firmly placed around my neck she pushed me into the wall with a final thrust and let me go. I smacked her hands away and glared at her. She smiled and turned on her heel and walked into her room. I closed my eyes and tried to tell myself that what just happened didn't.

I couldn't get any sleep last night. My mind kept spinning in circles trying to find a reason for Rebecca's behavior. I almost considered going to the landlord but realized that would mean having to go back home. The apartments were booked and there was nothing else available for seniors. I also didn't like the idea of having to be home and do classes online. That was just out of the question. I flipped through my pages as the teacher read aloud. I held onto every word said right up until the end of class. I did what I could to take my mind off Rebecca.

I was halfway through my salad at lunch when Carver came over to me and sat down at the table. She smiled at me and greeted me as if nothing happened yesterday. I guess, looking back on it, nothing did happen.

"I wanted to tell you earlier, but you look dead tired."

"Oh yeah? I couldn't get much sleep."

"So, are you going to tell me?"

I shoveled another fork full of salad in my mouth and turned to her and gave her a questioning look. She continued and asked me about what happened with Rebecca.

"I mean… nothing really happened. She was just upset about

something."

"Yeah, she seemed super pissed at you."

I thought for a moment about what to say since telling her I got choked out wouldn't be the right thing to say.

"Yeah, something of hers was missing from her room and I assured her I hadn't been in there."

I told her how her boyfriend comes over a lot and may have taken something. She seemed satisfied with that lie and left the subject alone. We talked about studying over her place next and that idea cheered me up. I wanted to know more about her and being invited over seemed like the perfect time to get to.

The dating pool for me in college was scarce. Despite being attracted to both sexes I never found anyone that I could really click with. There was never a spark of chemistry, no magical floating feeling, no butterflies. But every time I looked at Carver something would bubble up in my core and send spirals of pleasure through my veins. I thought love at first sight was something that existed in fairy tales. So, no way could it be happening to me, right? I thought about her smile and the dimples in her cheeks. I wondered what it would feel like to have my hand caressing her cheek and pulling her chin to mine where our lips would brush against each other gently. Like flower petals floating in the wind caressing one another and pulling away.

"Azlyn?"

I blinked a few times and tried to grab hold of what she was saying but I hadn't heard anything. "What's up?"

She laughed and shook her head. "I was asking if this weekend worked for you? To come over?"

Before my heart could burst from its chest I nodded and told her yes right away. She gathered her things and waved bye to me. I stifled the urge to fist bump the air and settled with a smirk.

# Chapter 7

## Rebecca

There weren't any clients in the clinic today, so I was bored shitless. I tried small talk with my coworkers but that ran dry. I scratched at my scrubs and spun in my chair searching for some excitement. I flipped through photos on my phone and ran across one with Shayna and me. She was so pretty. She had almond eyes, long black hair and smooth caramel skin. She got her looks from her Indonesian mother and African American father. I envied her complexion. My own was a pale and splotchy thanks to my white mother and African American father. Shayna had a slim figure in high school. I tried to imagine what she would look like now. Her breasts were probably still small and perky, and her hips spread slightly. I wanted to feel the jiggle of her cute butt in my fingers.

    I pushed my chair up close to the edge of the desk and spread my legs. I placed the tips of my fingers against the thin fabric of my scrubs and nudged my clit. I checked my phone to see how long I had before it was time to go home, and twenty minutes felt like hours from now. I rubbed my clit in small circles and slid my fingertips over my puffy lips. I could feel the heat of my sex so strong I almost forgot I even had on scrubs.

    "Hey, I need the chart for Lucy Smith."

    I looked up from my pleasurable escapade and saw my coworker hovering over the wall of the desk. With my mood officially ruined I handed her the chart that lay next to me and watched her grin and sprint off. I rolled my eyes and huffed. My phone vibrated from the back pocket of my pants, and I gasped as my pussy pulsed in excitement. I flicked through my notifications and found one from Adam saying that he was on the way to pick me up.

    I liked Adam but it bothers me that he doesn't want to meet my dad. I mean how else are we going to secure the inheritance if things don't move past the girlfriend stage? I expect a ring and a big ass wedding from this man. If I can't have that then why be with me at all. I shrugged off the irritation not in the mood for a fight and gathered my things to get ready to go.

When I arrived home Azlyn wasn't there. I wondered where the fuck she was since classes ended for her hours ago. I felt the irritation returning. Adam wanted to come in, but I lied and told him I was tired and wanted to go to bed early. I tried texting her, but I didn't get a response. I got angry and threw the phone down and it bounced somewhere underneath my desk. I stripped out of my clothes and decided I would take a shower to calm myself.

    As the water washed over my skin, rinsing away the bubbles, I let my mind drift back to that night. It was a Friday night and I had invited the class over for a party to reign in the spring. Music blared from my speakers. People were chugging beers, girls were twerking, and boys had their hands on their hips. The lights were low, and the air smelled of stale beer and sweat. I spotted Shayna coming in with another girl I didn't know. I knew her name and that we shared a couple of classes but nothing more beyond that. They were walking hand in hand until more of Shayna's friends showed up and swept her away. I couldn't tell exactly where her friend went and frankly, I wasn't interested enough to find out. But I should've been.

I danced for a bit with my friends and soon they all took off in their own ways. I made my way upstairs to make sure no one was making out in my bedroom. I weaved through the twerking, kissing and ass grabbing and finally saw my bedroom door. As I approached it, I noticed there was something going on in the room next door. The door was slightly ajar, and the moans of a young woman filled my ears. I started to step inside but what I saw when I looked towards the couple made my spine shudder and my skin crawl. I couldn't breathe. I couldn't think. My world came crashing down in mere seconds. I clenched my jaw and balled my fists around the doorknob as rage built inside of me. With a forceful tug I slammed the door shut and yelled for everyone to go home. The party was officially over.

I lay in bed that night with my thoughts pounding against my skull trying to escape my memory. I saw my Shayna sucking face with someone else. That someone else wore the same hoodie that her friend wore and bore the same chocolate brown skin. I knew it had to be Azlyn. I balled my fists up in my sheets and winced as tears pricked the corner of my eyes. My phone rang nonstop, but I couldn't hear anything over the pain in my pounding heart. I didn't go to school the next few days and my mother called in sick for me. I didn't know love could hurt this bad. When I found the strength to answer my phone it was from Shayna. I couldn't speak; I just listened to her plead and beg in my ear, with endless questions about how I was doing and what was wrong. She had the nerve to ask that after breaking my heart like this.

Thinking about it now, I never felt so foolish in my life. No one makes a fool out of Rebecca Cassidy Hall and gets away with it. I was hell bent on revenge and hell hath no fury like a woman's scorn. I ended up leaving the school and relocating for the second time in senior year. I thought I had made my mind up to move on and get over what happened but when I transferred here to Rosewood University and found out who my roommate was, rage boiled in me all over again. I vowed to make Azlyn's life here hell. No way was I going to let her live down stealing the love of my life away from me. I wanted to make her experience the humiliation and pain I felt that night. I just had to.

# Chapter 8

Carver's apartment wasn't far from the campus. I walked about ten blocks to reach it and was grateful for the elevator to take me to her floor. I found her apartment number and knocked on the door. I heard a stereo and TV blaring amongst side chatter. The hall was made of concrete walls and wooden doors. The lights overhead were warm and burned a light blue. When the door finally opened a skinny coffee-toned woman appeared with waist-length red hair. She was chewing gum and hooked her hands in the straps of her jean shorts.

"Can I help you?"

I tried looking over her shoulder and she positioned herself to block my view. I told her I was here to see Carver and she eyed me up and down before closing the door in my face. I grew anxious, fearing I had come to the wrong apartment, so I took out my phone to scan our texts and verified the address and unit number. The door then opened again, and Carver appeared dressed in a checkered shirt, black sports bra and black spandex shorts. Her hair was in a loose bun at the back of her head and loose curls framed her face. I sighed a breath of relief.

"Hey girl, come in."

She welcomed me in and introduced me briefly to the other guests in the apartment. She told me that the woman that greeted me earlier was a friend of hers named Lexi. As I followed Carver hand in hand into her room at the end of the hall, I could feel a set of eyes lingering on me. I wondered if they were Lexi's.

When we got to the room, she let me sit on her bed and I took out the books we were going to go over. She flipped through materials on her desk and came over and joined me on the bed with a pen and notebook in hand. We went over the book we chose for our class presentation and assigned topics to each other to present. I couldn't help but trail my eyes along her slender legs, her thighs and her stomach. It was flat and her belly button pressed inward. It was cute. Her dimples flexed when she spoke and smiled and she kept sweeping curls from her face when they would fall freely from her bun.

"Azlyn?"

I saw her mouth moving but I couldn't hear the words coming out. I wanted to know what she tasted like.

"Azlyn?"

She snapped her fingers in my ear and I shook my head to regain focus. She laughed and repeated her question. She was asking me if I wanted something to drink and if whiskey was fine. I nodded and she stepped out leaving the door slightly ajar. I got up and wandered around her room looking at the posters on her wall and small trinkets on her desk. I picked up her sweatshirt that lay draped across the back of her desk chair and inhaled its scent. It smelled of THC, and Lavender. I never enjoyed those scents before but after inhaling I felt a tinge of pleasure between my legs. I sat it down and went to the door when I heard Carver talking to someone. I stepped out and peeked around the corner and got a view of the kitchen. Lexi had her hands on Carver's hips and Carver had hers crossed over her chest. They looked like they were in an intimate discussion. Lexi kissed Carver on the cheek, and she smiled at her. I ducked back in the room with my heart pounding in my chest. I was confused and concerned.

Just as I sat back down on the bed Carver appeared with two

bottles of Whiskey. I felt alarmed in her presence instead of the calm I felt earlier. I swallowed and took the bottle she offered me. I took a few swigs and exhaled.

"Damn girl, you can drink."

I looked at the nearly half empty bottle in my hand and gave a slight laugh.

"Yeah I guess I do, everyone has a poison right?"

She smiled and nodded, taking down a few gulps of hers as well.

"So… " I began. I took another sip and asked her about Lexi. "So, are you and Lexi pretty close?"

She furrowed her brows and her cheeks turned pink. "I mean… that came out of nowhere."

She laughed and I smiled back at her waiting for an answer.

"I mean… I guess. Why?"

"Oh, um she just seemed pretty guarded when she answered the door."

She nodded her head. "Oh, that's just Lexi."

I nodded my head. We talked a bit more about the book and finished up our notes for the night. She turned on the TV and AHS came on. It was a crime thriller that we both ironically enjoyed. We watched a few episodes with our backs against her headboard. We were on our third bottles, and I began to feel a tingle in my lips. I looked over at Carver who appeared to be fine, but her eye lids were getting low. I didn't want to overstay my welcome, so I told her I was ready to head home. She offered to give me a ride.

"I mean it's just a few blocks. I'll be fine."

"No are you crazy? It's past midnight and you're tipsy. I'm driving you home."

"Really it's fine."

"No."

She took my hand and we marched outside to her car where she ushered me into the passenger seat and took her place in the driver's seat. When we peeled out of the driveway I laughed, and she looked over at me and smiled.

***

I stretched my back in the chair of Mrs. Valorie's office and took another glance at the forms before me. I had to alphabetize and file them in the client's correct folders. Mrs. Valorie had been in her office all day with phone call after phone call. Flashbacks to that day in the file room fluttered through my mind and warmth crept through my thighs. I didn't know how far she intended to take things with me, and I wasn't sure how long I wanted to stick around. She was good to me in every way but lately my mind has been elsewhere. Fantasies of Carver consumed my mind most of the day. We texted back and forth about how each other's day was going. She was bored at work since there wasn't many guests throughout the day. She usually worked nights but took a shift for a friend.

I was in the middle of texting her back when Val came over and sat on the edge of my desk. "Hey."

"Oh, sorry."

"It's fine. How are you doing?"

I thought about how to answer her and told her that I was doing fine. She asked how my classes were going and how my job hunt was going. I told her that I hadn't really planned for what happens after graduation. She scolded me and made me promise I'd start looking soon.

"Graduation is barely months away, Azlyn. You don't want

to end up back home, right?"

I shook my head. She put her fingers under my chin and pulled my attention to her.

"You must get on it. I have a few resources in mind but it's important you do the leg work."

I nodded. She sighed and told me about a phone call she just had with her husband. He invited her to dinner tonight and she was complaining about going in her work clothes. I reassured her that she looked fine, and he would be a loser if he thought otherwise. She smiled and lifted my hands to her mouth and kissed me. I could see the hunger in her eyes she was trying to contain, and a pit of curiosity and worry twirled in my stomach.

After work I made my way home and stripped out of my work clothes. I was ready to hop in the shower but when I turned around, I saw Rebecca standing in my doorway.

"Haven't seen much of you lately."

That was the point, I thought. I wanted to have bare minimum contact with her, so I had been staying out later at the library or hanging out with Carver.

She walked towards me and pushed me. I rolled my eyes and swiped her hands away as she reached out to me.

"Come on, stop."

I repeated myself to no avail as she kept pushing against me. Soon I had knocked into the side of the bed and sat down. Before I could stand back up, she had her legs on either side of me and her cunt was grinding into me.

"Stop playing around!"

She squished my face in her hands and placed a crude kiss on my lips. She bit my lip when I wouldn't return her kiss and I gave in. I kissed her back and she brought her hands down to my breast and gripped them. I wanted to get this over with. I bit her lip back and she reached a hand up to slap me.

"Behave."

Too stunned to respond, she kissed my lips and caressed my breast. She picked up one of my hands and placed it inside of her panties and made me fondle her clit. She gripped my hands firm and rubbed herself to her heart's content. She moaned and bucked her hips back and forth grinding deeper into my fingers. She gripped the back of my neck and pressed my lips against her collar bone. I kissed her and she let out a few swears. She tucked my fingers into her soaking wet hole and rode my fingers up and down and warm juices slid down my fingers and puddled in my palm.

"Fuck."

She threw her head back and forced two fingers deep in her hole and with her free hand she clutched onto my left breast, digging into my skin with her nails. I gritted my teeth trying to brace myself through it and kept telling myself over and over that it would be over soon. I bit my lip and swore to myself as pleasure swelled inside me as her moans rang in my ear. I hated myself for getting aroused and cursed my body for betraying me. She moved her hand up from my breast and wrapped them around my throat and squeezed. I struggled to breathe, and my gasps seemed to excite her more. When she could thrust no longer, she let out a cry and collapsed onto me. I yanked my fingers away and she pushed me down away from her. She began laughing to herself and walked away. A feeling of guilt, disgust and pleasure danced in my core.

After she left, I laid back on my bed and thought about what just happened. I didn't know how to process how I felt, so I did what I did best and shoved the thoughts away. I got up and yanked a towel off the back of my chair and stormed my way past her room and into the bathroom to shower.

It took a lot of hot water and soap to get her scent off my fingers. I scrubbed my exfoliating sponge over my skin vigorously desperate to remove any leftover residue of her from my pores. I felt invaded by Rebecca. I held my breath and stepped into the running water so that it drenched my face in its warmth. Water trickled down my arms, tripped down my nipples and spiraled down between my legs. Her moans still rang in my ear. I cupped my breasts and let the water wash over them. My hands slid down my belly and parted my lips. Water raced down my fingers and brushed against my clit. Pleasure surged inside of my womb. I exhaled.

# Chapter 9

## Carver

When I wasn't in class, I spent most of my time picking up shifts at Mama's Bar and Grill close to the campus. I've been working there since freshman year and Mama and I grew close. She treated me like I was her own and picking up the extra work was more than enough to pay her back for all of her love and support throughout the years. I straightened my apron and was about to slip my phone into my pocket when I got a text from Azlyn. She told me that she had a good time with me. I put my phone in my locker and headed out to the main floor. I had a good time with her too. She laughed a lot, and I liked her smile. I kept wondering to myself which way she went but figured it wasn't something I should be concerned about. I figured she was bi or at the very least curious. Gay girls had a way of sensing these things in other women. I wondered just how far her curiosity went though. Azlyn was about 5'2, thick with a bit of meat on her bones and had these cute plump breasts. I didn't want to work myself up before my shift, so I stared at myself in the mirror and regained my self-control.

    I circled the bar looking for empty glasses and paid attention to those customers wanting refills. Hours ticked by and empty glasses flew. Drinks were spilled and some couples argued amongst themself. I was wiping down the bar when a tall, blonde and older man came in and took a seat. I got them started with cups of water until they requested something stronger. I overheard them discussing some business deal and watched him stroke her inner thigh. She tried to push his hand away, but he gripped her harder and she stopped resisting. I chucked him up as another pig preying on a young woman. The next couple was an older man and his wife. They ordered glasses of scotch and talked about the golf game that was playing on the screens.

Hours ticked by and soon it was time for me to clock out. I greeted the next shift supervisor and headed to the check in room to turn over my tips to Mama.

"Hey, doll."

"Hey, Mama, I made 250."

"Oh, that's what Mama likes to hear."

We talked about how the night went and who came and who went. We talked about how school was going and what plans I had afterwards. Just the common chatter with Mama. Shortly after she let me turn in for the night.

Before heading to the breakroom to change out of my apron I was grabbed by Oliver, one our busboys.

"Hey C, you never got back to me. I know you have some fine ass friends you can hook a brotha' up with. Don't lesbians bang— I mean hang together or whateva'?"

I rolled my eyes and playfully pushed him away.

"Boy, is you stupid? I told you all of my friends are gay. And even if they weren't, you would surely turn them out."

He staggered backwards clutching his chest in fake disbelief. I shook my head and headed to the back.

Lexi had messaged me a few times, forgetting I don't carry my phone around at work. The bottom line was that she wanted to see me after my shift. I weighed my options and sighed. Somewhere in me I knew I could muster up the energy. Her legs were sculpted by the gods and her taste was warm honey dripped on my lips. I bit my lip and made my exit out the back door.

I arrived at my apartment close to midnight. I fumbled for my keys in my bag when I felt a set of long fingers trail down my spine and a deep hum against my neck. The scent of coconut and shea butter wafted through the air and I knew I had been embraced by Lexi. I grabbed her wrist as it began wrapping around my waist and pulled her in front of me pressed against the now closed door. She breathed heavily as her eyes darted searching for mine in the darkened hall. I closed my eyes and inhaled her scent, bringing my mouth to her neck and kissing her tenderly. She gasped and tugged on my shirt pulling me closer. I gently bit into the crease where neck met shoulder and felt her shudder through my core.

"Fuck, C."

I hoisted her up by her thigh and felt her silken flesh that lay bare to the touch beneath her skirt. My fingers toyed with her clit and slid down into her hole. She moaned and I covered her mouth with my hand and began kissing on her chest. Two fingers deep and she was clutching onto my back pulling me closer. I trailed my tongue down her neck and with my free hand I stroked her nipples through her sheer top. She moaned in my ear and clutched me until she came with the force of gods. I stuck my fingers in her mouth and she licked them clean. I could tell she was grinning at me in the dark. When she was finished, she kissed me and took the keys from my hand to unlock the door.

***

Lexi lay naked next to me on her back smoking. I took a few hits and passed it back to her.

"What do you think of her?"

"Of who?" I didn't know who she was talking about for a second but I took a guess. "Azlyn?"

I took her silence as a yes and thought for a moment. I didn't think much of her besides she was attractive. Something in me stirred when her smile flashed across my mind. I grinned.

"She's cute. Innocent."

Lexi glared at me and snatched the blunt back. "Innocent my ass."

"You sound jealous."

"Of what? Her? Please."

I rolled over and caressed her left breast. She didn't so much as moan or push my hand away.

"Don't be playing with me, C."

I smacked my lips. "I thought you liked when I play with you?"

I let my fingernail slide down her chest and I clutched her mound with my hand.

"You know what I mean. When are you going to take me seriously?"

She winced and put the blunt out in the nearby ashtray. She rolled over and pushed her ass against me. I moved my hand up her hip and clutched her left cheek.

I rolled my eyes. Here we go again, I thought. Lexi and I had been seeing each other off and on for years now. She always hooked up with some guy and when things would end bad, she'd come crawling back to me. How could anyone take a woman like that seriously? Her mood changed with the wind.

"We've been through this before, Lex."

I let go of her and rolled over onto my back and tucked my hands under my head.

"Me and you could really work this time."

"For how long? Until another Drew or Tyler or whatever comes around?"

She stayed quiet. I wasn't saying anything either.

"It won't be like that."

Yeah, this time, I thought. She says that every time, but we always end up back here.

"Yeah."

I felt her stir next to me and next her hand made its way between my legs. I grabbed it and pulled her closer to me. I pressed my knee between her legs and parted them. My hand looped under her arm and I pulled her closer to me with my hand pressed against her back. She kissed my neck and I sighed. Her nails dug into my chest and I bit down on her shoulder.

"Ah!"

She moaned in my ear and I let my hands dip between her legs. She was warm, wet and inviting. Her lips found mine and we kissed with our tongues rolling around each other. I would bite her lip and she would shudder. I let my three fingers slip inside of her and curl around her g-spot. She gripped my arms and gasped in my ear. I let my mind wander away and found Azlyn's face in my head again. I imagined it was her I had my fingers inside of me and I bit down on her shoulder to stifle my own moans.

"C-C-C—"

She moaned my name over and over and again my mind turned to Azlyn. I wanted to know what she looked like with my fingers buried deep inside of her. I wanted to know what kind of pleasure would paint her face. I sighed and lost myself in my thoughts. I hardly noticed when she came, and she pulled herself off my fingers. She kissed my lips, but I didn't return it. She didn't notice as she rolled over and draped my arm across her waist. I was exhausted myself. Soon we both drifted off to sleep.

# Chapter 10

Spring break was approaching with graduation holding onto its ankles. I had plans for neither. I met with my counselors a few times to talk about my plans after college. Most of them asked if I wanted to continue my education while others encouraged me to start applying for jobs. Imagining me at some 9 to 5 wearing skirts and high heels with a bun pinned to the back of my head seemed a lot better than grinding the day away with mountains of essays and book reports. I was nervous and excited all at once about leaving this life behind and opening doors to the next one. Simultaneously, however, I was anxious for what that next life would be like.

    I left my apartment as quietly as I could trying not to disturb Rebecca. I didn't want to run into her sooner than I had to. I made my way to my philosophy class and let my mind be taken over by Aristotle and Socrates. We talked about Aristotle's view on friendship and love and how he viewed friends as people wishing good things for each other and how love can be explained in three different ways. One being desire for one another, the other being a deep appreciation for one another and finally the love exchanged between man and its God. We were to think about the types of love we've experienced in our life and whether we agreed with Aristotle's breakdown or not. I personally didn't know what to think. I agree that love is composed of desire and the fondness of another and there should be a distinction between the way man loves each other and the way man loves God. One, after all comes from the body and the other from the soul. I thought about the different ways I have experienced love and decided that maybe those ways weren't love after all. The desire was there. The well-wishing was there. But neither were strong enough to last. So, I decided there had to be a certain strength between these types for it to be considered love.

After class, I made my way through the lunch line and found a seat in the shade. I had avocado toast, green tea and a salad. I was taking a few swigs of my tea when Rebecca came over and sat across from me. I closed my eyes hoping I was seeing things but when I reopened them, nope still there.

"What do you want?"

"What are you doing for spring break? I know you're not going home."

I hadn't thought about my spring break plans but I also didn't want to share them with Rebecca of all people. Being alone in the room with her for four days was a recipe for disaster.

"I don't know. I'll be spending time with friends."

"Pfft. What friends? Anyways, there's a party tonight and you're coming out with me."

"Why would I do that?"

"Because." She crossed her arms and stared into my eyes. "If you don't? You'll end up being the most talked about slut on campus."

"Why would you do that?"

"Are you coming or not?"

She raised her voice at me, and I backed down. Trying to prevent a scene in the lunch hall. I rolled my eyes and swallowed my pride.

"Fine."

"Awe, then it's settled, babe. See you tonight."

I wanted to slap her. I wanted to scream. But what good would any of that do? I didn't want that rumor going around right before graduation. That's not how I wanted to be remembered. I sat back in my chair and folded my arms across my chest. I felt cold fingers on my shoulder and looked up to see Mrs. Valorie staring down at me with a smile. She sat in the seat next to me.

"I saw what happened… is everything okay?"

"Oh. Yeah everything is fine; just some roomie harassment that's all."

"Roomie harassment?"

"Everything is fine, Val."

"It didn't look fine… "

"Please, can we drop it?"

I didn't want her prying into my life. I didn't want to shatter whatever precious image she held of me in her mind. I didn't want her to know about the torment from Rebecca. I had things under control right? Right?

"Look… I know we never really talked about what happened between us the other day but—"

"Oh please, Val. Isn't it a little late for that?" I clenched my jaw thinking my tone was a bit off. I wasn't in the mood for this. "I'm sorry. But what more is there to discuss? You relapsed. It happens."

"I don't mean to compare you to a drug—"

"Not me. This." I motioned to the space between us.

"I'm sorry."

"Val. Let's not do this, okay? I'm here for you no matter what but now just isn't the time to talk about it. Look I have to finish up my classes for the day."

"Are we okay?"

I thought for a moment and sighed. "We're fine."

I headed out first and dumped my trash in the bin by the door. It looks like I was heading to a party this evening.

***

I decided that going to the party wouldn't be that bad and that I needed some fresh air and a change of surroundings anyhow. I chose to go with a simple black tank top dress and some ankle boots. Something quick to slip in and out of would always be my go-to.

On our way there, she decided to vent to me in the car about how things were going between her and Adam. I just remained silent the whole way. I knew we were close to the house when I could feel the vibrations of the music thumping throughout the car. Rebecca let out a few "ooos and hell yeahs" as excitement creeped into her. When we parked, I couldn't wait to get out of the car. I felt the weight of an elephant step off of me as I stepped out and made my way to the porch. Rebecca caught up with me and hooked her arm through mine and ushered us inside. I let the beat of the music pulse through me easing my anxiety as I gazed around at the drunk and too happy faces. I may have been the only one there that would rather be at home.

As the music started Rebecca hips moved against me and she pulled me onto the dance floor. I didn't think our night together would include this. I did my best to keep up with her awkward rhythm or maybe it was just my uncomfortability. She laced her hands around my neck and looked past me, a smirk growing on her face. I followed her eyes and saw Adam perched against the wall with guys talking clearly at him and not to him. His eyes were watching Rebecca while his hands clutched a beer. He looked away, tossing the beer in a nearby can and went upstairs.

Rebecca smacked her lips and followed him.

Grateful to be released from Rebecca's grasp I made my way to the kitchen and rummaged through the fridge for anything other than stank beer.

"Looking for this?"

I lifted my head and saw Carver perched on the door of the fridge holding two Jack Daniels. I grinned and grabbed one from her. Suddenly excitement swelled in my chest. When I closed the fridge, I saw that she wore some tight fitted jean shorts and a red halter top. The red was a compliment to the hazel in her eyes.

"Where did you come from?"

I thought it was a dumb question, but she had a habit of drawing out my thoughts through my lips before I processed them.

"I know a guy who knows a guy." She smirked.

We sat on the bottom of the staircase and people-watched for what felt like hours. She told me about the DJ, the cook, the host and how the host was a friend of her sisters. I didn't know she had a sister. Her hair was curled and pulled into a loose bun; her gold earrings dangled against her puffy cheeks. I desperately wanted to lean in and kiss her but held myself back. I was losing my mind. There was no way on earth that would smooth over well. Oh sorry, I just landed against your face with my lips. No.

"Ugh. You make me sick!"

"Me? NO, it's you! All you want to do is argue over bullshit. I'm sick of it, B."

"Yeah? Whatever. Piss off!"

A drunk woman staggered down the stairs next to me making barely an effort to excuse herself. When my eyes met those long shapely legs, I realized it was just Rebecca. Nothing new with her, was there?

"Ugh, fucking asshole."

Part of me felt like I should chase after her; after all, she was my way home, but I sat still and watched her push through the crowd and out through the front door. A few girls giggled and a few guys looked annoyed.

"Wasn't that—" Carver started.

"Oh, um yeah. It's fine. I mean she did bring me here but now that I think about it, I'll be better off letting her have her space."

"Yeah, I mean she's totally loaded. Is it even safe for her to drive?"

"Rebecca? Yeah, she's fine. She's mostly just pissed, but I've seen her more intoxicated than that driving just fine."

She laughed and shook her head.

"So, how did you get here?" She stole my question from earlier.

"Um, you just missed it."

"No, way. She drove you?"

"Yeah… "

"Annnd you just let her leave… without you?"

"Oh. Well fuck."

We laughed and I put my head in my hands. I didn't think that part through clearly.

"Come here, dance with me, girl." She led me onto the dance floor.

I could see that Carver was excited to be here, so I tried my best to manage. Her grin stretched ear to ear as she bobbed her head to the track. I laughed awkwardly watching her dance beautifully. I also wasn't much of a dancer, so I stood there just gazing at her passionately. I more so enjoyed lurking off to the sides watching the crowd, being the center of attention was never my aim. Carver embodied the role. Her hips swung and her chest swayed; she was enjoying herself. Her eyes never left mine. She motioned for me to join her, but I immediately froze in place. Everyone was either blinded by the lights or too drunk to care but I couldn't dance to save my life and the thought of being watched was agonizing.

    She laughed and pulled me close to her. She grinded her hips against me and trailed her hands down my arms and snaked them around my waist pulling me into her. She felt up my back bringing me closer, and her lips pecked against mine. She searched my eyes for a question she already knew the answer to and leaned in to kiss me again, this time deeper. I sighed against her mouth as pleasure swelled inside of me. Before long I found my hips matching in rhythm with hers and as if possessed by her spirit I couldn't stop. She was a love drug, and I was afraid of the fall.

    It felt like I had been dancing for hours once we finally decided to head back to the staircase. My hips felt stiff and sore, but my face was full of laughter and light. She left to get us some punch from a punch bowl, and we toasted to absolutely nothing. A few drinks in and she checked in on me to see how I was enjoying the night. I was honest. I told her about my fears and hesitations and how they melted away when I danced with her. I asked her why did she kiss me and she told me it looked like I needed it. I wanted to tell her that maybe I needed it again, but her friends showed up and she began chatting away with them. I fumbled through apps on my phone wanting to shrink myself inside a hole and hide and just then Carver wrapped her arm around my waist making sure I didn't go too far in that hole. My heart thudded against my chest over the noise of the crowd, over the noise of the music and over her conversation. I felt a nudge against my ear and realized she had been calling me. She pressed her lips against my ear hoping I would hear her better. Oh, I heard her alright. All of me did.

I turned towards her, and she stood up offering her hand to lift me up as well and we made our way through the crowd, following her friends. I felt like I could follow her anywhere. My heart began to swell as I gazed at the back of her head and watched her look back at me grinning ear to ear, her cheeks a rosy mess.

Just when time began to stop, I felt a hand on my shoulder, and I was yanked away from her after we made it to the door. She frowned and I looked to my right and realized it was Rebecca. I thought she had left but apparently while I was distracted with Carver, she slipped back inside. My world felt as if it had turned on its heels. She turned my face towards hers and placed a crude kiss on my lips. I tried to push her away but her grip on me was tight.

"Rebecca, what the fuck?"

"No, you what the fuck! I saw you hung over that bitch. Are you kidding me?"

"Bitch? Who the fuck are you talking to?"

I noticed a red-head step in and hold Carver back. The red-head looked at me and winked.

"It's okay, baby, let's go. Let's just go."

She laced her fingers through Carver's and pulled her out the door.

"Let go of me."

"No. We're going home."

"Rebecca!"

I heard Adam's voice calling somewhere over the music and Rebecca took off with me firmly in tow and we made it to her car. She pushed me inside and sat in the driver's seat and locked the doors. She huffed and puffed as we sped off down the street with the music fading to a point of non-existence.

"I don't know what the fuck you think you got going on, but it ends now."

"What the fuck are you talking about?"

She gave me a look that sent chills down my spine. I cowered in my seat and tried to think of a rational way I could get out of this situation. But no words came to my mind. I was only left with the burned image of Carver's upturned face glaring back at me.

"Who was that?"

"Who was who?"

"Don't play dumb with me."

"Carver, my fucking friend Carver."

"And you were just gonna go off without me? I brought you here. Who the fuck is she to take you away?"

"Why do you do this? Why are you so fixated on me? What the fuck did I do to deserve this?"

"Don't act like you don't know!"

"I don't that's why I'm fucking asking!"

"SHAYNA COLE!" she yelled over me.

I shook my head confused and it took me a moment to process what she said.

"Shayna Marie Cole. My best fucking friend for years that you snatched right from under me."

"What are you talking about I don't know—"

"Yes, the fuck you do know!"

She put her foot back on the gas and we sped off towards our apartment. I racked my brain trying to figure out what Shayna had to do with any of this and it hit me. I recalled kissing her in a moment of passion at a party we went to in high school but I also remember the door being shut so how did Rebecca know? She must've popped in at some point. I balled my fist.

"So what? We kissed. What's the big deal?"

"Are you being serious? The big deal is that she was mine! You took her from me!"

"I didn't take anyone from anyone. If she was seeing someone, I would've known. She was my friend too."

"Bull shit she was! You preyed on her. You filthy fucking dyke bitch! You preyed on her and swept her away from me!" Rebecca slurred her words together and swerved the wheel each time she glared at me.

"She clearly didn't want you and frankly I can see why!"

"What the fuck did you just say!?"

Rebecca swerved the wheel a little too far to the left and we rushed into the other lane.

*BAM!*

She couldn't see the truck coming towards us. I couldn't stop her.

*Screeeeech!*

The car plowed into the truck, and we spun several times before coming to a stop just off the side of the road. My head spun and hit against the dashboard. The last thing I remember was seeing Rebecca's head slam into the air bags and her body go into a blurry limp.

# Chapter 11

## Carver

I pushed Lexi off me and made my way through the crowd and out the door. By the time I reached where the cars were parked, they had already sped off. I swore and kicked the ground. Lexi and the others caught up to me and kept asking me over and over about what happened, but I didn't know what to say. I barely knew what to think. Why did she kiss Azlyn? Why did she drag her out like that? What the fuck do they have going on? I put my hands on my knees and took a few deep breaths to regain control over myself.

"Let's go."

Lexi put her hand on the back of my shoulder, and we began walking towards my car.

"What was that about?"

We had made it inside the apartment. Chris and Lauren were talking amongst themselves in a corner of the living room and Lexi was standing over me. I swirled the beer around in my hand and took another swig then set it down.

"I don't know. Quite frankly I shouldn't care. Whatever they have going on I don't want no part of it."

"Judging by the way you kissed her earlier I doubt that."

I rolled my eyes and looked up at her.

"If you have something to say, say it or leave it alone." I snapped.

She looked unphased and sighed. Lexi stepped closer to me and got down on her knees. She began kissing my knees and making her way up my inner thigh. She looped her fingers in the hem of my shorts and looked up at me.

"Let me make you feel better."

"I'm not in the mood," I lied. I was hardly ever not in the mood for Lexi.

She yanked my shorts off along with my boxer shorts. She dipped her head down and licked along the slit of my sex. I winced and spread my legs farther for her. Her tongue snaked along my lips and looped around my inner folds. She kissed my clit and licked along the rim of my hole. I gasped and clutched hold of the cushion of the couch as she dipped a finger inside of me and wrapped her lips around my clit and began suckling on it. Gasps turned to moans as my breath quickened. Thoughts swirled in my mind about Rebecca kissing Azlyn and Azlyn pushing her away, all the way to the kiss Azlyn and I shared. Her lips were soft, and buttery. Her fingers scratched and rubbed against my walls and her tongue pulsed against my clit. My head began to shake, my fingers sore from gripping the cushions to tightly. My legs were trembling with an impending urge to climax. I picked my left leg up which was a mistake given that she now had better access to work her tongue along my clit. She pulled back my flesh that surrounded my clit and lapped her tongue along its center. I nearly screamed with pleasure. I convulsed and gripped her head with my other hand forcing her mouth to suck me deeper and deeper. I shivered and let out a series of 'fucks' before erupting in ecstasy. I sighed and she finished me off by slurping up my juices.

"You bitch," I gasped out.

She straddled my hips and we kissed.

***

In the blink of an eye spring break was over and another week was at its end. I made my way through the glass doors of Mama's Bar and Grill and headed to the back to change into my apron. Once I was finished, I gathered some ice to restock the bar and began arranging bottles in their proper place. Shit day shift should've done. I shrugged it off. I needed the distraction. I hadn't heard from Azlyn all week. She hasn't answered any of my texts or calls. Our project was due next week and I wanted to at least finish that up if nothing else. But still, no word.

"What can I get you today?" I asked the kid sitting across from me scrolling through his phone.

"Um, Bourbon?"

I fixed him up a glass and carried onto my next few customers. Sometime in the evening a group of guys came in and sat at the bar. I got them their drinks and cleaned up the rest of the bar area. I was sweeping when I heard one of them talking about Azlyn and some car wreck.

"What?"

They stopped and stared at me in response to my question.

"Uh what's up?" one of them asked.

"I—I'm a friend of Azlyn's. Did you say something about a car wreck?"

"Oh um yeah, it happened last weekend, after that party. Car was wrecked pretty bad."

"Fuck the car— I—How is Azlyn?"

"They're not letting anyone in to come see her, so I haven't been able to check."

"Fuck."

I rubbed my temples and sighed. What the fuck did she get herself into. I did my best to finish up the rest of my shift and made it to my car. I debated whether it was worth going to the hospital or not since they weren't letting in visitors. I decided I would just head home and wait for her to contact me. When I got there everyone was in their own rooms for once.

I made my way to my room and stripped to shower. My mind wouldn't turn off. I heard the chime of my notifications go off and hopped out of the shower hoping it was Azlyn. It was. I had a missed call and a text from her. She was apologizing for not contacting me sooner and for missing all of my calls and texts. I skipped over all of that and just asked how she was doing. She decided to call again so I sat down.

"Hey, I'm sorry again."

"Don't be. I just want to know how you're doing. I heard."

"Yeah… I'm honestly still trying to wrap my head around it. I just got a few scratches and a mild concussion."

"What happened?"

"I don't know… one minute Rebecca was screaming at me about something and the next there were these bright lights and all I remember after that was waking up in the hospital."

"Damn. This is so fucked up. What the hell was she thinking? I shouldn't have let you leave with her."

"It wasn't your fault."

I didn't know what else to say to her. I suppose I should ask about Rebecca, but I didn't really care to know. I asked her if I would see her in class this week and she told me that she hoped to be out of the hospital later today. She wanted to see me as soon as she could. I told her to let me know when she was out so that I could pick her up.

## Chapter 12

It was the first weekend after the wreck. Minus a few scratches I was visibly fine. It turns out that Rebecca had swerved into the wrong lane and an oncoming car braked before crashing into us. Rebecca's side was hit the hardest and she hasn't woken up yet. I was asked if I wanted to see her, so I did. She looked... peaceful.

When Carver pulled up to my place and turned the engine off, she asked if I was alright. I told her I was, but she told me I had been clutching her hand tightly the whole ride. When I finally released her hand mine was stiff and cramping. I can't imagine how hers might've felt.

"We can go back if you think it's too soon—"

"No. I—I'm fine."

She got my door for me, and we walked into my apartment. I tossed the hospital items into the trash and headed into my room. I missed my bed. I stripped down into my tank top and panties, laid down and clutched my pillows. I sighed.

"Do you want me to go?"

My eyes flew open and the realization that Carver was standing in my doorway hit me. I had forgotten she came in with me. I felt silly for being half naked and exposed. I sat upright on the bed and turned towards her with a pillow in my lap.

"No—Um—No."

She put her jacket on my desk chair and sat down on the bed with me.

"Look... I know it's not any of my business but what is

going on between you and Rebecca? I mean… you didn't look so happy to leave with her."

I pulled the pillow closer and sighed. I wasn't sure where to start. I wasn't sure if I even wanted to start. I guess the best thing to do would be to just start. I told her what happened when we moved in and how she overheard me masturbating and has been tormenting me ever since. I told her about what happened in the bathroom and what happened in the car. She was quiet through most of it and just looked at me. I looked away afraid to meet her gaze and discover what kind of judgement lay there. The conversation Rebecca was having with me in the car came back to me now. She seemed to get the idea that I took Shayna away from her and that bothered her because she had a crush on her. Carver reassured me that none of that gave her the right to do the things she's done to me. She asked me why I didn't try to stop her or report her but I didn't know what to say.

"You can't keep letting her put her hands on you. You have to do something about it."

"Like what? It's not like there's somewhere else I can stay. Senior year is almost over, and I thought… I thought I could just bear it until then."

"Do you really not want to go home that badly?"

"Going back there isn't an option for me."

She paused and it looked as if she was debating on asking me something, so I tried to fill in the pieces.

"My parents were my first bullies."

She waited for me to continue.

"I was never thin enough, smart enough, respectful enough. I talked too much. At nine years old dressed in a uniform skirt and tank top apparently made me look like a slut. Too much skin exposed." I shook my head and kept going. "I can't go back there.

They don't want a gay slutty daughter and I don't want bullies for parents."

She sat quietly and looked down at her hands then continued. "I want to do something for you. I want to help you."

"I don't need your pity, Carver. I don't need you to be my savior."

"Well, you need someone!" She sounded more aggressive than I'm sure she meant.

I looked down at the pillow and bit back tears I didn't know were there. "I've been managing on my own for twenty-four years now. I can manage a few more." I mumbled.

She sighed and took my hands in hers. "Azlyn."

She searched my eyes for answers to an unasked question. I looked at her and suddenly regretted this whole conversation. I didn't like sharing this weak and vulnerable part of myself with anyone and I certainly didn't expect to share it with Carver.

"I'm pathetic, I know that."

"That's not true. You've just been through... a lot."

I looked down at her hands. They were soft and strong. I felt like I could curl up inside them and all my problems would go away. But that's not how the world worked. I knew that.

"I should get going."

I didn't want her to leave just yet, so I didn't let go of her hands. She didn't bother moving either.

Carver gazed at me for a while, and I turned away unsure of what was running through her head. Maybe she was thinking about how pathetic I was for letting people run over me for so long. I was so afraid of my parents and being forced to go back home, that I let myself get manipulated by Rebecca. Just then I felt the tips of her fingers touch my chin and lift my face up to hers. She had scooted closer to me. Before I could respond her lips had melted against mine and her hands slid down my shoulders lifting me into her grasp. My head felt dizzy as her tongue waltzed across my lips and mingled with mine. I moaned out in pleasure as she bit into my bottom lip and gripped my waist. I wanted to get lost. I wanted her to take me away to a place of pure ecstasy. My doubts, my fears, my worries all ceasing to exist in this moment of bliss. When her lips left mine, they drifted over to the left side of my neck. First her tongue pranced across my skin, and she placed a gentle kiss where my neck met shoulder. By this point moisture was seeping between my legs and I yearned for her touch. I let the pillow fall to the floor.

"Tell me to stop," she begged but I refused her plea.

Her lips met my collar bone, and her fingers found my nipple and pulled. I whimpered in pleasure, and she asked me over and over begging me to tell her to stop. I refused. I parted my legs and leaned back as she mounted me. Her hands tucked inside my panties and slid them off. She placed her knee in my groin and I rocked my pelvis against her. I whimpered yearning for her touch.

"Come on, Az. Tell me to stop."

I shook my head and her lips met mine again as her fingers forced themself between folds of flesh and teased my little nub. I cried out breaking myself from her grasp and moaning as pleasure consumed me. Her fingers were magic. Wet, slippery honey seeped from my pores and doused her fingers as they found their way inside my little hole. Her lips hooked onto my neck and her free hand firmly gripped the sheets beside me. I moaned until I felt a wave wash over me and I shook. I have never been touched this way before. I let several 'fucks' escape my lips, but not once did I tell her to stop. I couldn't. It was too late. All of me was in her grasp and I wouldn't dream of having her let me go. She bit my shoulder and I shuddered.

"Please, please, oh fuck, fuck, fuck, fuck"

I braced myself but a surge of pleasure gushed from my core and washed over me. I gasped for breath as she bit into my shoulder harder. I begged for her bruise, her kiss, her touch. Her fingers pulsed quicker inside of me. I felt my juices pouring out of me and sliding down her fingers. I gasped louder and swore until I convulsed for the final time and climaxed in her grasp. She pulled her fingers out of me slowly and tasted them. She moaned and placed them against my tongue, and I licked them clean.

"Good fucking girl."

I nodded and sucked on her fingers making sure I got every drop. This was a part of me I had never felt or seen before. My body craved her and only her. I felt hypnotized by her presence. I couldn't move; I couldn't think. I had drowned.

Her lips found mine again and we embraced each other. I took off my tank top and melted my lips against hers once more. Carver stripped down as well, and my fingers fondled the flesh between her legs. My lips found her pink soft nipples and I nudged the right one with my tongue. She moaned and bit her lip leaning back against the bed. Her legs lifted and wrapped around me. I kissed down her stomach and traced her bellybutton with my tongue. I pushed her legs apart gently and worked my tongue between her folds. I lapped at her clit and nudged against her hole with the tip of my fingers. I trailed my tongue down her flesh and up again tasting her juices as it dripped out her hole. She was sweet and bitter all tangled into one delicious flavor. I fondled her hole with my tongue working my way inside of her and my thumb pressed against her clit gently in small circles. She fidgeted beneath me and moaned with her finger pressed between her lips. I slid my tongue back up to her clit and slurped at her juices. She dug her palms into the sheets and bucked beneath my grip. I held onto her hips and continued suckling her juices until she convulsed in my grasp. Her chest heaved and began to slow down in deep breaths. I kissed her lips a few times and licked up her juices. She pulled me up to her and we kissed. She licked my lips tasting herself and I moaned against her mouth.

When things calmed down, I rested my head against her chest, and she wrapped her arm around me. Our legs lay intertwined, our hearts in sync. When I closed my eyes, I no longer saw flashes of light or heard the screech of tires. All I felt was her skin against mine and all I could hear was her breathing. It was slow, and gentle almost as if she didn't want to disturb me. I felt calm in her grasp.

# Chapter 13

## Rebecca

The faint sound of machines beeping called me out of my slumber. I yawned and stretched my arms above my head only to feel the tug of IV needles and bandages. I rested my arms at my sides and blinked my eyes open. I was in a white room with tan furniture and a couch with blue cushions. My walls were part glass and overlooked a reception desk. I realized I was in a hospital. My senses snapped into gear as the scent of alcohol wafted through my nose and the cool breeze from the overhead air vent ruffled the hairs on my arms. I could almost taste the saline that swam through my veins. Distant chatters and phones rang from somewhere outside of my room. I looked around frantically, searching for some clue as to why I was here. Just then my parents came in the room, and I felt a sense of calm.

"Oh honey!"

My mom rushed over to me and embraced me. My dad rested his hand on her back and held his face solid to block out his mixed feelings. He was probably doing his best to mask his pain and anger.

"You must tell them what happened! It was that girl, wasn't it? She did this!"

I coughed a few times before trying to speak. "What are you talking about?"

My mom began explaining to me what happened that landed

me in the hospital. She explained the wreck and that me and another girl was injured. Every time my eyes closed, I saw flashes of light and heard the screech of tires. I tried to recall what happened, but my memory felt blocked.

"Who was I with?"

This time my dad spoke with disgust in his voice. "That Ashlyn or whatever the hell her name was. She yanked the wheel, didn't she?"

I sat quiet for a moment trying to recall what happened. We were having an argument. I remember my voice feeling hoarse and my head pounding. I was yelling at her. She was yelling back but I wasn't paying attention to what she was saying. When I looked back towards the traffic a truck was heading towards us. I stepped on the brakes but by then it was too late, and we collided. I swerved to the right trying to get back into my lane but that just made the impact against my side of the car more intense. It was me, I thought. I caused the wreck. I wasn't paying attention to the road. I didn't dare speak. My parents began discussing the details of the insurance and involving lawyers and I let my mind drift away. I stared out the window trying to imagine myself far away from here. But there was no escaping. Not now.

***

The next day, I was discharged from the hospital. I went back home with my parents and rested in my room. I checked my phone and went through it answering all the voicemails, text messages and social media outreach of how are yous and where are yous. I only had several missed calls and texts from Adam. I wasn't sure if I was in the mood to see him, but wouldn't all girlfriends want to see their boyfriends when something like this happens? I texted him back telling him I was at my parents. Not too long after that he was pulling up and being let in by my mother.

"Baby!"

He rushed over to me and embraced me in one of his bear hugs I used to love so much. He kissed all over my face and lips. I decided I would let him have this moment and I relaxed into it.

"I was so fucking worried, man."

"So, this is what it takes to get you to come home with me and meet my dad?"

"Your dad isn't even here. He stepped out."

I rolled my eyes. Always the smart ass.

He collected my assignments for me while I was out and told me that my teachers gave me another week to finish them. They couldn't offer much more since finals week was damn near tomorrow. I sighed. As if I needed any more stress. I had clinicals and exams to worry about. I asked him if he had been back to my apartment, and he told me did but since I wasn't there, he stopped visiting. He told me about a strange car he'd see there every now and then and how one of the bedroom lights were on, but no one ever answered the door. I figured that must've been Azlyn. I guess she made it out of the wreck. Part of me was disappointed.

"Tell me about it."

"NO." I sounded more irate than I meant to be. I softened it by holding his hands. "I'm just done talking about it. That's all I've been asked to do since I woke up."

"Right. Right. My bad, B."

We sat for a moment in silence before he decided he needed to take off. He was just stopping by to see me before meeting up with the guys. His shitty ass couldn't even spend the night? I rolled my eyes and waved him off me. He held back his irritation and just told me I needed to get some rest and left.

Later that night I went down for dinner. Somewhere along the way the conversation changed from how business was going to how I was doing after leaving the hospital and rested on what I wanted to do for school. I immediately thought about transferring out, but I was literally a couple of weeks away from graduation. I couldn't leave now. My mind drifted to thoughts of Azlyn curled up in bed with that slut Carver and I grew more irritated by the second. I wasn't finished with her yet either.

"Cassidy, you must finish your classes here. You are weeks away from graduation and the party has already been planned remember?" My mother pleaded to me, and I rolled my eyes. I hated hearing things I already knew repeated back to me.

"Your mother is right, Cas. We've invested too much money into this year for you to throw it all away now."

I slammed my fork down and got up from the table. My parents didn't even look phased.

"Settle down now, girl."

"I'm sick of this!"

"This isn't like in high school! You can't just pick up your shit and run off like some little girl!"

"I'm not saying it is! I don't want to be there anymore!"

"You have to be an adult now, Cas. The world isn't like Mom and Dad. It isn't so forgiving out there."

"Screw out there! You're supposed to have my back!"

"Not when you're disobeying us and causing wrecks!"

If my dad's skin were a shade brighter his face would be beet red with anger. He knew. He knew all along that it was me. That I caused the wreck. Blaming that little twat would've been better than believing the truth about his own daughter.

"Fuck this."

"Excuse me?"

I screamed and stormed out the front door. I didn't know where I was going but I knew I didn't want to sit at that table for another minute. I walked over to my car and hesitated. My hands began to tremble as I reached for the door handle. Was I ready to get back on the road? Annoyed with how shaky my hands were, I kicked my tire and pulled out my cell. I called Adam demanding that he pick me up. He kept asking questions, so I just hung up on him and sat on the porch to wait. I could hear my parents bickering amongst themselves. My dad wanted to charge after me and my mom was pleading with him to give me space. I didn't know where I wanted to go but I knew I didn't want to be here listening to their bullshit.

When Adam pulled up, I told him to just get me out of there. We ended up at a park we used to go to when we wanted to spend time together. He was reminiscing about the good days and asking me what went wrong. I didn't know how to answer him, so I just kissed him. He pulled me onto his lap, and we kept kissing until I couldn't breathe. Thoughts of Azlyn wafted through my mind with each touch he placed on my body. When his hands would grip my hips, I thought about Azlyn's fingers sliding into me. When his lips painted the side of my neck, I thought of Azlyn's lips. I was confused and conflicted. I didn't know what I wanted anymore. I pushed him off of me and stared back at him. He was confused but relaxed when I let my hands explore his chest. I was determined not to let this moment go to waste thinking about Azlyn. Why her? Why now? Why like this? He gripped my breast and pinched my nipples. I grasped onto the frayed ends of pleasure and turned a blind eye to her face blaring in my mind. Fuck. Fuck her!

## Chapter 14

It felt as if we were the only ones in the room. Presenting next to Carver I couldn't feel the eyes of the students on me or the glare of the teacher. I focused on her words, her mouth, that same mouth that caressed and touched my sensitive places. I caught myself grinning and struggled to keep a straight face. Carver saw me and her eyes fell to my lips as I spoke. She took my hand and we bowed and as if a curtain had lifted, I could see the faces of the crowd. We took our seats and the teacher passed us our grade. We both passed. I looked over at Carver and beamed! She felt my excitement. Her hand found my inner thigh and she held me. We smiled at each other and it felt as if everything in my world was falling into place.

"See, I told you everything would be fine."

Carver and I walked hand in hand to a table in the dining hall with our plates.

"I was so nervous."

"Really? You looked calm to me."

I took a bite of my salad and watched Carver stir hers.

"You weren't kidding about loving meat."

She laughed and I watched her toss her pile of meat around in the lettuce.

"Have you thought about what you're going to do after graduation?"

I bit my lip. Coming from anyone else I would've been annoyed about being asked for the millionth time about my post-school plans. But from some reason I felt safe with Carver.

"Yeah... Mrs. Valorie told me about this Therapist assistantship that's opening this summer and hiring new graduates."

"That's amazing, Azlyn! You know I'm rooting for you."

"What about you? I know the bar is your baby but will you stay there forever?"

"I don't know... there's this gallery taking new work and I'm considering sending them some of my work."

I nearly dropped my jaw. I had no idea she was into art. I mean I noticed the work around her room but I had no idea it was her work.

"Carver, that's incredible! I want to see more of your work."

She bashfully turned her fork around in her salad and I let my knee slide between her legs. She smiled and her knee knocked into mine and I knocked back. We laughed and she took a bite of her salad.

"How many classes do you have left today?"

"Just one."

"Come over after... and I'll show you some things I've been working on."

I bit my lip and gazed at her tongue as she licked her lips. She cupped my face in her hand and brought me close to hers and planted a kiss on me.

"Carver... "

She kissed my lips silencing me and I nearly knocked over the glass of tea that sat on the edge of the table. I cursed myself for being so clumsy. We laughed and parted. We finished our meals and went off in our own ways.

\*\*\*

"I can't get over how talented you are. When's the

deadline?"

I sat on Carver's lap as we browsed through her digital catalog on her laptop. I was helping her select different artwork to send to the gallery. I was blown away by the realism in her work. It felt as if I was looking at a photographers portfolio instead of 2D work.

"It's in a couple weeks."

"Omg, Carver, you have to get on top of this thing. Send them in now."

"What like right now?"

"Yes!" I giggled and she leaned her head on my shoulder.

"You really think these ones are good enough?"

"Good enough? Carver, these are fucking amazing. I honestly thought these were photographs. You have this way of…" I let my fingers slide across her lips as I looked into her eyes and continued. "This way of capturing the true beauty of a woman."

She gripped my hips and pulled me closer and our lips touched lightly just as we heard someone burst into the room. I gasped and Carver frowned and looked towards the intruder.

"Lex? What the hell?"

"C! He fucking… he fucking… "

She began sobbing uncontrollably and I got up off of Carver's lap. She rushed over to Lexi and in a blink of an eye they had disappeared out the door leaving me alone and confused. Carver had left her phone so texting her was no use. I didn't know what to do so I sat down in the chair and tried to wrap my head around what just happened. Just then Carver dipped back into the room.

"I'm sorry, I have to deal with something."

"I—Carver! Slow down what happened?"

"Look I can't talk about it right now."

She kissed my cheek, grabbed her phone and keys off the desk and left again. I held my arms biting back sudden tears. What the fuck just happened? I called Drew and got a ride home from him. He asked what was I doing outside of campus and I told him to mind his damn business. Considering he was kind enough to give me a lift I decided I shouldn't pick a fight.

"I was visiting a friend."

"Mhm. I see. They got you all in a bitchy knot I see."

I smacked my lips and propped my knee up and leaned against the window. What was that all about?

"Hey… Drew, do you know this chick named Lexi?"

"I'm perfectly fine with you coming to me about your relationship problems but tell me she isn't the next thing on your to-do list?"

"Omg, shut up. It's not like that."

He paused for a moment as if looking off into the distance before he continued.

"We were a thing about a year or so ago. But we broke things off. She was a total head case. She always wanted to show off with me. Like she had something to prove to someone. I wasn't vibing with that at all."

"What happened?"

"I ended things with her. She was always hungry for attention from other guys or hell even girls."

I nodded my head.

"Do you know if she's seeing anyone now?"

"You really got a nigga curious. Why do you care so much?"

When I didn't answer he continued.

"Yea, I guess. Some dude named Malcom or whatever. He's a little bit of an ass but aye it don't got nun to do with me. You shouldn't pry into it either."

We parked out front of my apartment. I hugged and thanked Drew mostly for the info than the ride home. I figured maybe something happened between her and this Malcom guy. Carver and Lexi must be pretty close for her to come bursting in crying like that. Part of me felt annoyed. I wondered if this is what it felt like to feel jealous. I locked the front door behind me and grabbed a glass of wine from the kitchen. I headed towards my bedroom but something in Rebecca's room caught me off guard. There were boxes where her bed was supposed to be and most of the things in her room had been packed away. I went back into the living room and noticed the TV and couch she had moved in were missing as well. The feeling that washed over me was pure confusion. I sat the glass of wine down and left the building. I crossed the street and knocked on the Apartment Manager's door. Her light was on so I knew she was still in the office.

"Hey, Mrs. Brooks."

"Oh my god! Azlyn, I'm so glad you're alright!"

She squeezed my shoulder and leaned back against the doorway.

"It's a shame what that girl did. Getting drunk and driving like that. No wonder you guys crashed so hard."

"What... how did you—?"

"Oh, sweetheart, we all know. Someone recorded the whole thing, and it was reported to the school. That girl is lucky she's not expelled."

My mind was swirling with a cocktail of panic and relief.

"But you don't have to worry about her anymore. She's been evicted from the premises and has to continue her classes online from home."

Part of me should feel relieved. I was relieved right? I mean

I wouldn't have to face her anymore. Her touch, her taste wafted through my mind and a knot formed in my stomach. There was no way she was taking this well.

"Thank you, Mrs. Brooks."

I headed back home and plopped down on my bed. Suddenly I burst into a fit of laughter and sighed holding my sides. It was over. Everything I had been through with her. It was over. I wouldn't have to deal with her touching me anymore or the harassment. That was one less thing I found I had to worry about with graduation approaching. I stripped out of my clothes and took a hot shower. Instead of getting dressed when I got out, I let myself air dry as I waltzed around the apartment with a near empty wine glass in my hand. For a moment all of my cares, and worries melted away. It was over.

# Chapter 15

## Carver

When I woke up, I was laying in bed with my arms around Lexi. Panic settled in and I tried to recount the events of last night. I remember going to Lexi's apartment. It was a mess. It looked like the cops had raided the place or something. I asked her what happened and that's when she unloaded everything on me. She had started seeing a guy named Malcom a few months ago and hadn't told me about it. This made me question everything she told me the other day about how a guy wouldn't come between us again. I knew there was no "us" but I still felt betrayed. I swallowed my emotions to hear the rest of the story from Lexi. It turns out Malcom had a temper and lashed out when she didn't do things the way he liked or if she went out without him. He never hit her, but he did destroy her place trying to figure out where she was going these past few nights. I take it she never told him about me or how close we lived to each other.

"Lexi, you realize how in-fucking-sane this is right?"

"I know man. I know. I messed up, C. I messed up."

"Where is he now?"

"That's not the point. I hadn't been answering his calls and I hadn't been to his place in a while. I just got fucking bored man. I was sick of it."

I shook my head. Of all the people and times for her infamous boredom to creep in. She explained to me how sweet he was when things were calm between them but I just waved that off. It was a matter of time before his anger turned on her and he began putting his hands on her.

"Look. You're gonna pack your shit and stay with me for a few. Alright? Chris and Lauren are moving out so I'll have a spare bedroom. But for now the couch will have to do until after graduation."

"The fucking couch? Why can't I just sleep with you like before?"

When I didn't respond she rolled her eyes in disgust and dropped her bag of clothes.

"It's because of that bitch, isn't it?"

"Hey, watch your fucking mouth!"

"I'm sorry, C. I'm just upset. I need you and you have your nose up some other girl's ass."

"That other girl has a name. It's Azlyn. She has nothing to do with this."

She sat down on the bottom of the stairs after packing her bags and I sat next to her.

"What am I going to do, C? He's going to find me."

"Look." I sighed and tried to grasp the situation. "Look. We're not going to think about that."

I didn't really know what I planned to do. I knew my home wouldn't be the most perfect of havens, but it was better than having her getting targeted by Malcom. I told her that she needed to end things with him properly and I would be right beside her to help. The last thing we needed was her ghosting him and him tearing up the city looking for her. I told her to start from the beginning and explain to me when things changed between them. She told me that he gave her too much attention. He always wanted to be up under her, and she felt like she couldn't breathe next to him anymore. Those were definitely things we were going to leave out of the breakup conversation. The last thing we needed to do was damage his ego anymore than what she's already done.

By the time I made it home Azlyn was gone. I texted her asking how she made it home and I hopped in the shower waiting for her response. I was thankful when she told me a friend picked her up instead of hearing she had walked. We weren't far from campus but something in me saw her as something to protect now. When things with Lexi calmed down I made her some of my famous hot chocolate and we curled up on the couch. She had stopped shaking and crying.

"Lex… "

"This is good."

I smiled and paused before continuing. "I like her… Azlyn, I mean. I like her."

I closed my eyes as this school girl rush of emotions washed over me. Her voice pulled me out of my haze.

"I can tell. Why else would you be moving her in? That's it right? That's why you won't let me sleep with you anymore?"

I bit my lip and slowly nodded my head. For the first time it was me that was choosing someone else over Lex. I wondered if this was how she felt when she chose other men over me. When I looked up she had rushed over to me and planted a kiss on my lips before I had time to react.

"LEXI!"

I pushed her harder than I meant to and she hit the arm rest. She winced and scowled at me.

"What?"

"Try something like that again and you're out of here!"

"Fuck you!"

She bit her lip and I could see tears pricking her eyes again. I rolled my eyes.

"Look… " My voice softened. "It's late. I have to get up early to practice for graduation. If you need anything let me know but let's just get some sleep, OK?"

I got up and disappeared into my room without looking back to wait for her response. I heard her scoff as I closed my door. I lay in bed scrolling through my phone and realized Azlyn had been checking in on me. I let her know I was heading to bed and would see her tomorrow. I must've fallen asleep and somewhere in the middle of the night Lexi snuck into my room. I slid myself from under her and decided I would talk to her about this later.

\*\*\*

I shuffled through the crowd of girls taking selfies and made my way to the check in desk. I checked in and waited by the desk for Azlyn. When I saw her dark hair pulled up into a bun, her black t-shirt dress that revealed her brown legs and plump cleavage I bit my lip and watched as she took her name card. We hugged and found a place in line. We both wanted to be near the front so that our wait wouldn't be too long for us to cross the stage. We practiced how we were to enter the gym, cross the stage and exit the gym. Shortly after the practice we met with our class in the dining hall for mimosas and brunch. I noticed that Azlyn seemed to be looking around the room more than usual. I took it that she must be looking for Rebecca. It could've been a rumor, but I heard she wasn't invited to the brunch. I took Azlyn's hand in mine and kissed her fingers. She blushed and took a sip of her mimosa. Some of my other friends joined us at our table and I introduced Azlyn. She didn't get to properly meet them at the party. She smiled and mingled with them quite easily. They were picking fun at honor students who took their turns giving speeches to the class. I laughed with them and downed my mimosa. I turned my attention back to my friends when they began discussing details of the after graduation party that was to take place at the football captain's house. I looked over at Azlyn who was working on her third mimosa and seemed interested in the talk about the party.

"What do you say? Want to come with us?"

I looked over at her and searched her eyes for the yes that was vying to breech her lips. She nodded her head and giggled. I took the pitcher from her and wondered if she knew what she was agreeing too.

"I wanna go. I want to be with you, Carver."

Something about the way she said my name sent tingles down between my legs. I bit my lip and as if she could read my mind she placed her hand along my inner thigh and squeezed. I clutched her waist and clenched my jaw doing my best to stall the hunger that was building up inside of me for her.

"Azlyn… "

"Yes."

She answered a question I didn't have to ask. I bit my lip and she leaned over and planted her lips on mine. I didn't expect such a deep and inviting kiss in public. I enjoyed this newfound confidence of hers. Did I have this effect on her? I kissed her back.

# Chapter 16

Graduation was days away. Mrs. Valorie was busy all morning and afternoon with calls to families and back to back making sure their kids were ready and had solid plans for when school ended. When counseling with her ended. I was putting the final touches on Mrs. Valorie's website and set up a booking platform students could pay for so they could continue their counseling if they wanted to over the summer. She leaned over my shoulder and made comments on my progress. She liked it so far and wondered why I didn't major in programming. I told her the math and coding part wasn't my thing.

"Are you ready for adulthood, Azlyn?"

She leaned over my shoulder and turned her face towards me. When I looked at her, I realized her lips were dangerously close to mine. She smelled like jasmine and rose water. I backed away and she noticed my retreat and stood up.

"I mean… I guess I kinda have to be."

"That's right… "

She reached down and slid her hand down my cheek and cupped my chin in her fingers to turn my face to look up at her.

"Val… "

"You've been so distant lately. What's up"

She caressed my cheek and I closed my eyes and swallowed. I imagined my heart beating slowly and controlled my breathing.

"Look… I'm seeing someone."

I opened my eyes hoping to see her beautiful smile but I was met with a face twisted in confusion.

"What do you mean you're seeing someone?"

She took her hand off my face. She crossed her arms and looked down on me.

"I mean exactly what I said. Aren't you happy for me?"

She blinked a few times and huffed. She began pacing around and shaking her head.

"This is insane, Azlyn. You're about to go off and start a career. You shouldn't have your priorities mixed up."

"My—my priorities mixed up?"

I was baffled by her response.

"Yes. This is a crucial time for you. You're finally leaving home and facing the real world. You're going to go out on your own and make something of yourself. You can't be held down by some boy."

"Some boy? As if it's any of your business her name is Carver. She's not holding me down if anything she's been an inspiration."

She scoffed and looked at me as if she was scolding her child.

"Aren't you going to be happy for me?"

"No. Azlyn, I'm not. You can't even stand on your own two feet yet and you're getting yourself sucked into some relationship now out of all times. Now. Hours away from graduating??"

"I don't understand. Why are you being like this!"

I rose my voice and felt her hand brush sharply against the side of my face. It stung like a wake-up call. She put her hands up to her mouth and began profusely apologizing. I made my way to the doors before she grabbed my wrist and spun me around to face her. I smacked her hand off of me. I was too stunned to speak. I felt a tear fall down my cheek.

"Azlyn... I'm sorry. It's just, I feel like I've helped raise you in some way and I don't want to watch you fall backwards."

I swallowed and did my best to keep my head held high.

"It's none of my business. I shouldn't have hit you. I just... the idea of losing you it... I just... I just want what's best for you."

I let my eyes fall to her hand she used to caress and strike me and back to her face.

"You don't get it, Val."

"Then explain it to me."

I sighed and searched my brain trying to figure out where to start. I began with how I never felt whole or worth anything from the moment I admitted and owned up to my sexuality to Shayna. I told her about how we kissed out of curiosity. It was Shayna's idea to get me to kiss her as a way of promising I'd be forever true to myself and true to her as my friend. I told her about how Rebecca spotted us that night and how that sparked all of the torment I endured from Rebecca up until the car wreck. She was stunned and speechless. I told her how I met Carver and how things blossomed between us. I told her how for the first time in a long time I felt in control over my life. With Rebecca gone and with school being almost over I would soon be free from my parents. Things were finally falling into place for me and I felt weightless. By the end of the explanation, I found my joy again and the sting had left my face.

"I'm happy, Val. Really happy."

Her face twisted as if she was going to ask me something but decided to swallow her question. It was for the best. She reached out to me, and I flinched. She embraced me and I let myself dissolve in her grasp. I knew she was only looking out for me, and her emotions had got the best of her. I forgave her.

After work, I made my way back to my apartment and noticed that there weren't anymore boxes in Rebecca's room. The whole place was empty, and I could hear my voice bounce off the walls. I decided to invite Carver over. While waiting for her to come over I grabbed two glasses of whiskey and set them out with a plate of fruit I knew I wasn't going to eat.

When I heard the knock at the door I grinned from ear to ear.

"Hey."

"Back at you."

She had bottles of whiskey in her hand, and I ushered her into the room.

"Okay… I'll bite. Why this room?"

"I just want to kiss things with Rebecca goodbye once and for all. I want to make good memories here."

She set the bottles down and looked around.

"I mean... if it's too weird we can go back into my—"

She pressed her lips against mine and pushed me gently against the wall. I guess things weren't weird after all. We kissed until my lips grew sore and I turned away leaving her to place her lips down my chest. I moaned as she pressed her knee between the folds of my flesh and slid me over to the backside of the door. Her teeth sank into the left side of my neck as her hands twisted and pinched my nipples. I slithered my hand underneath the hem of her dress and tucked her panties out of the way. My fingers danced over her clit gently nudging the small nub free of its delicate skin. She moaned as she kissed my neck and pinched my nipples harder. My fingers flexed faster as moisture seeped from her pores. I parted her lips further and trailed my way to her small hole and dove two fingers deep in her crevice. She cried out and with her free hand found my clit underneath my panties and pushed them aside. I was already soaking so slipping her fingers deep inside my hole was effortless. Her fingers dove deeper as mine hooked and rubbed the ridges of her silky walls. Her tongue twirled circles along my chest. I ached to be consumed by pleasure. I bucked and twisted, my body unsure of itself and my mind too intoxicated to focus. We moaned in breaths begging for air but unwilling to let go of eachother.

    By the time my arousal reached its peak we had stripped out of our clothes and pressed our bodies into each other. We made our way down onto the rug in the center of the room. Underpowered by her mouth that trailed from my breast and suckled on my hips, the floor was forgotten territory. I craved more and parted my lips with my fingers as she made her way to my clit. She suckled and lapped at the pools of honey slickening my folds. She shoved finger after finger inside of me followed by her tongue lapping up the moisture at my entrance and trailing back up to suckle on my clit. I cried out at her touch unable to silence my moans and groans. I caved at her will and allowed my juices to flow down her fingers and puddle in her palms. She licked her fingers clean and crawled up to me. I could taste my juices on her lips as I kissed her and licked up every drop. She straddled my face and hovered herself over my mouth. I brought her hips closer and licked the juices flowing out of her. She moaned and shifted her hips back and forth sliding herself across my tongue. I moaned refusing to take in air as she bucked against me. I let the air leave my lungs as waves of pleasure rolled over me. She leaned back and I kissed and sucked on her clit. I dove my tongue into her hole desperate to taste her rigid walls. I let her bounce up and down taking my tongue as deep as it could reach inside of her. She bucked back and forth intoxicated with pleasure and no longer hearing my gasps for air. Tears pricked the corner of my eyes as I took in sharp gasps of air through my nose. I inhaled her scent and felt myself gush with pleasure. I reached up to grab hold of her ass and held her in my grasp. I licked against her walls and twirled my tongue inside her picking up every bit of juice I could that seeped from her walls. She cried out and held my head against her body smothering me in her flesh. I grew dizzy and drunk in ecstasy. I didn't want this moment to end. I didn't want to come up for air. I wanted to drown. She yanked my head back as she squirted wall after wall of liquid pleasure. I laughed and rubbed her clit with my free hand as her body jerked away from me.

"Damn girl."

She gasped and took a moment to regulate her breathing. I didn't let her have her moment too long before I was straddling her hips and had my lips locked around hers. She pulled me off her to look into my eyes and when her lips met mine again something felt different. The kiss felt deeper; her moans felt purer. I wondered if this is what it was like to fall for someone. I sighed against her and poured myself into her.

# Chapter 17

## Azlyn

I moaned and rolled over. I wasn't ready for my night to end and day to begin.

"Azlyn."

I felt someone hands slide between my legs and lips meet the side of my neck.

"Azlyn."

I blinked myself awake and stretched.

"Carver?"

Her lips melted against mine and she quickly pulled away.

"We're gonna be late if we don't hustle, girl."

"Fuck, says the woman that fucked my brains out all night."

She laughed and pulled me to my feet. We began getting ready for graduation and met up with the rest of our class in time to line up at the entrance to the gym.

"Please stand and welcome our class of 2022."

We followed in line all the way to our seats. The president of the college gave his speech followed by the dean and others. When it was time for us to walk across the stage, we handed our calling cards to the speaker and walked hand in hand to the edge. When I felt that leather case in my hand it felt as if the whole world was watching. I barely noticed my parents in the stands calling out to me. My mind was set on moving forward.

After the hat toss and escort out of the gym we met up with

our families for photos and hugs. I stood awkwardly by Carver and her sisters.

"Elena, this is my girlfriend. Azlyn, meet Elena."

I bashfully stuck out my hand and was embraced by the tall red head followed by her younger sister Lori. She introduced me also as her girlfriend to her parents who were unphased and just as excited to meet me.

"Soo. Girlfriend, huh?"

"What? Too soon?"

"No, no it's fine it's just that… well I didn't plan on introducing you to my parents. I didn't plan on interacting with them at all actually."

"That's okay. You can when you're ready. But since they're here they're going to want to know where you are, Azzie."

Wow a title and a nickname all at once. I bit my lip trying to quiet the rise of energy in me.

"It's just that they… "

Before I could finish, I was stonewalled by my parents coming up behind me. Shit. They found me sooner than I hoped. I had two seconds to make up my mind on whether after twenty-four years I was going to come out to my parents or risk damaging a blooming relationship. But as if she saw the racing thoughts spilling out my mind and the panic that drenched my heart she leaned in close and kissed me and in that moment nothing else existed.

"Carver?" I managed to ask when she pulled away from me.

"You're an adult now. Own up to your truth. I'm right here."

I turned around and let my eyes fall upon my parents. I walked over to them and stood waiting for their harassment, their firing of slurs and curses.

My dad was first to speak. "I've always known—"

"Oh, shut up you didn't either."

My mother cut him off and fired off a round of slurs and curses telling me how much of a disgrace to God I was. I felt as if I was a thousand miles away from here. On a completely different planet while my hands rested in Carver's.

"I don't care."

"You and this tramp better not ever set foot in my house."

"I don't plan to."

"You no good mother fucking whore. God will punish you! You are a blemish in his sight child."

"You're not hearing me!" I snapped and she hushed herself. I looked at Carver who had an amused expression and didn't look at all phased by her words. "I'm not going back with you all. That place has never been home to me. I'm an adult now and I can make my own choices. If you don't want to respect that then I don't want anything to do with you."

My dad just sulked in silence and my mother exchanged glances from him to her expecting him to respond but I knew he wouldn't. He was weak in that way. He reached his hand out and pulled me in an embrace and I felt my strong exterior crack. Tears welled up inside of me and he just held me tight.

"You're right. I don't approve. But I will always love you and you're always welcome home," he whispered to me before squeezing me one last time and letting me go.

I looked over at my mother who fumed silently. For once, she had nothing more to say and I was done listening anyways. I turned to Carver and kissed her back as a big fuck you to her and we took off back towards her parents who were ready to say their goodbyes and head back home.

\*\*\*

It wasn't until we got in the car headed to the party that I felt the weight of my actions. Even if I wanted to go back home and there was no bone in my body that did, that option was dead to me. I propped my legs up and leaned against the door. Carver took my hand and kissed my fingers. When we pulled up to the house the lights were off and for a moment it felt as if we were at the wrong address.

"Is this it... ?"

"Yeah, it must be. There's cars all parked around."

"Well let's go check it out."

She got my door for me and we went up to the porch. We rang the bell a few times but then I noticed the door wasn't closed all the way and we could let ourselves in. We did just that and walked around the dark and quiet living room for a while looking for signs of life. Then it hit us. There was a steady pulse coming up through the floor. I bent down and pressed my ear to the floor and heard the faint sound of music and muffled voices.

"Basement?"

She nodded to me and we made our way down the hall and found a door in the kitchen. We entered the narrow stairwell and was hit with a full blast of music and screams. We closed the door behind us and proceeded down the stairs and into what could best be described as the main area. We waded through the sea of bodies and figured we had found the party at last.

"Oh my god."

"I know right?"

Carver put her hands on my hips and helped me sway to the rhythm in tune with her hips. Soon her lips found mine in the darkness peppered with strobe lights. I kissed her lips and she tugged on my bottom lip. I moaned against her mouth and let the rhythm sweep me away into an endless Carver filled bliss.

"C!"

"Hey!"

"Hey, C!"

She pulled away from me and was embraced by a group of her friends. They chatted away and I stood there awkwardly until Carver looped her arm through mine.

"Remember these guys? My old roommates?" She spoke so close to my ear I could feel her lips brush against me softly.

I nodded my head and flashes of last night crept into my mind. Her touch, her taste, her voice dripped into the forefront of my mind like nectar.

"They want to know if you want a drink?"

I nodded again and she pecked my lips and laughed. I watched as her friends took off towards the bar area and to grab us drinks. When they returned someone else had joined them. I locked eyes with a tall blonde haired brown skinned woman and a chill went down my spine. Confused I shook my hips to wiggle out the odd feeling and Carver pulled me closer. I recognized the blonde as her friend Lexi despite the hair change. She didn't look happy in the slightest to see us together. She walked over to us ignoring the dancers around her as if she were untouchable and approached Carver. She suddenly started sobbing yet not a single tear dropped.

"Hey, what's up?"

She whispered something to Carver and Carver looked over at me.

"Hey babe, I have to take care of something really quick. Dance with these guys for a bit please," Carver quickly whispered to me before being ushered off in the direction we came by Lexi.

I did as Carver said and danced a bit with her friends until they decided to break away. Probably from my horrible dancing, I thought. I went and sat in a bar stool over by the bar and scrolled through my phone. There wasn't anything particular I had to look at until an idea came to mind. I pulled up Lexi's FaceChat and scrolled through her profile. She made a lot of posts about some guy and how he left her heart broken. She also made a few more, full of pictures with Carver and heart emojis. I couldn't help but feel a knot being formed in my chest. Why did she keep interrupting the time I shared with Carver? What did she really want? Was it Carver? I asked for three tequila shots and took them down the hatch and followed them up with the free juice the bartender offered me. I decided I would take my mind out of places it didn't belong. They had been friends long before I came around so surely whatever was going on wasn't even about me, right? I let the beat of the music thump my thoughts away.

# Chapter 18

## Carver

She stopped crying by the time we made it to the living room sofa and sat down. I found a light switch to a lamp and turned it on then sat with her. I let her gather herself for a few minutes and I stared at her to make sure she was done crying but instead I noticed her face was still dry. Were there ever tears? I wondered. I pushed the thought away.

"Tell me what's going on?"

She sniffed a few times and sighed.

"I just don't know what to do. I heard he's looking for me. If he gets his hands on me, I… I… "

She put her face in her hands and began heaving. I put my hand on her shoulder to calm her nerves.

"Look, it's going to be okay. What does he think you even did? Like why is he hunting you down?"

"I don't know! I mean… We had slept together one night and then I told him about how the next day I hung out with Josh and he just freaked out."

I let her catch her breath and calm down some more.

"He just, wont let me go anywhere or do anything if it's not with him. I can't even have friends. It's suffocating."

"Has he ever put his hands on you?"

"I mean… there was a time when he grabbed my throat really hard and shoved me against a wall and I don't know."

Something in me began to question the information she was telling me. I just felt deep inside that something wasn't adding up. There was something about this guy that she wasn't telling me. Or maybe it was something about her.

"Where is he?"

"I thought I saw him downstairs and that's why I got so freaked out. Like fuck he found me."

"Okay."

I got up and headed for the basement door and she grabbed my hand.

"Wait, no. What are you doing?"

"I'm going to go confront him and see what's got you so up in arms?"

"Wait… I mean. Can't you just sit here with me. I need you, C."

She laced her fingers through mine and pulled me towards her. I pulled away and reached for the handle of the door.

"Look if he did something to you, I need to know."

"I… I… "

Just as she started to say something I heard someone rush upstairs. As the door opened, she tightened her grip on my arm and hid behind me. I looked up and it was Malcolm.

"Fuck girl. There you are. You got me running all over town trying to see you."

"Stay away from Lex Malcolm."

I stood firm at 5'8 next to his 6'2 frame.

"What, what's up with you, man?"

"I know what you've done. You can't expect me to let you come near her. Look at her; she's frightened!"

"Aye, I don't know what you thinkin' I did but you need to back the fuck up."

"She told me all about the way you trashed her apartment and how you've been hunting her down and not letting her be around her friends."

"What? I ain't never even been to shawty's apartment. We're always kickin' it at my place or Mack's spot."

"How do you expect me to believe that?"

"You don't gotta believe shit. The proof is right there. I only been running around town lookin for her because she's been dodging my texts and calls. I'm tryna make sure she's good."

"Well, she is."

"Aye, say something to yo' watch dog. What the fuck is up with shorty?"

We both looked at Lexi who just stood there with a glazed expression on her face. I shook her hand and she looked at me.

"He's talking to you. Tell me again what he did to hurt you?"

"He… he had his hand around my throat and he was yelling and I thought he was going to hit me."

"Aye, what?! You trippin' big time, Lex. You know damn well I've never laid a hand on you like that!"

"It's true!"

"If I did then prove it. Where's the bruise huh? Big ass hands like these you better know they'll leave a bruise!"

He barked back at Lex and I felt her tense up behind me. At this point I didn't know what to believe. He had a point. He was a large guy with big hands. There would definitely be a bruise and there wasn't one. I looked at Lex for an explanation and for the first time I saw tears actually form in her eyes.

"Let's just go, C. I can't do this. I can't be around him."

"Be around me? Yo, I can't be around you! Fuck you too if you believe anything outta her mouth!"

He disappeared back into the basement. I turned to Lex.

"What the fuck, Lex? Are you being straight with me?"

"It doesn't matter, baby. He's an asshole; you can't believe him."

"I honestly don't know what to believe."

I started for the basement door, and she grabbed me.

"You know you want me as bad as I want you. Stop kidding yourself with that girl."

"Stop with the bullshit, Lex. I've had enough!"

I forced the door open and pushed her aside. I stormed down the stairs to go and find Azlyn. I had had enough of her shit. I went over and saw Azlyn and the bar talking to some guy. At that point in time all I wanted to do was scoop her up in my arms and run like hell out of there.

"Azzie!"

I rushed over to her and pulled her face up towards me and kissed her, disregarding the fact that she was in the middle of a conversation. When I pulled away she had that starry gaze that I loved so much.

"What was that for?"

"Oh, I just missed you."

She shook her head and introduced me to her friend Drew. I had seen him around but never really knew his name. He seemed like a decent guy and a little funny looking with a skinny nose and big ears. But he was handsome all the same.

"Let's go, babe."

"Already?"

"Yeah."

She kissed me again.

"Where's Lexi?"

"I don't know. Gone I guess."

"What happened between you guys?"

"She lied. She's been lying this whole time. She fed me some bullshit about Malcolm assaulting her but there's no bruises. She wasn't even crying real tears."

"Why would she do something like that?"

I paused for a moment trying to gather my thoughts. I knew Lexi still wanted me, but I never imagined she would stoop so low.

"I don't know."

I knew Azlyn knew I was leaving stuff out but all I wanted to focus on right now was getting home. I wasn't in the mood to party anymore.

# Chapter 19

I had begun to put graduation, Rebecca, school and studying behind me and was on the road moving forward with Carver. It's been a month since I began applying for jobs and I had only received rejection letters so far. The reality of adulthood began to dip its claws into my chest and hold on tight. Carver seemed distracted ever since we left the party, but I didn't want to pry. I'm sure whatever was going on with her and Lexi would resolve itself. They were friends after all I guess.

It felt weird being in Carver's home with no one else around. Her roommates had all gone home or started new lives elsewhere for the summer. I wondered how she was going to keep up with the rent but she told me that her landlady had been a childhood friend of her parents and they were pretty close. I guess that meant she wouldn't have to worry about it. Lucky, I thought. I still felt odd about just staying here knowing Carver was forking out rent money every month and I wasn't doing much to help so I began working at the bar parttime. I would come in on the weekends and mostly bus tables or help in the dish pit. I preferred helping out in the pit over bussing tables. At least that way I could keep my mind off of Carver. Off the way she smiles extra hard at the women that came in. I didn't want my mind to go there but with how much distance she had been putting between us it was bound to make me curious. The last time we really and I mean really touched each other had been the night before graduation. We would flirt with each other in passing and peck each other on the lips but that initial bubble of excitement I felt had begun to dwindle. I hadn't known her long enough to believe she was my everything or anything like that, but I did know her long enough to crave her very existence in my core at the same time. I felt like I was being pushed away or maybe all of this was just in my head.

"Azlyn... Azlyn?"

I blinked and realized Carver was standing next to me. The front of her shirt was wet and she was drying her hands on her apron.

"Oh, yeah sorry, what happened?"

"Did you miss all that?"

She laughed and told me that a woman had bumped into her as she was coming over to me and spilled her drink. I definitely didn't notice any of that happening just a few feet away. I was absorbed in my head.

"You gotta stay out of there."

She poked my head and wrapped her arm around my waist.

"Ready to go?"

I nodded and we made our way to the car. I couldn't take my eyes off of her chest that bounced more vividly beneath her damp, tank top. I bit my lip and paused when we got to the car.

"What's up?"

"I... am I still what you want?"

"What?"

"You know what I mean... "

I looked down at my feet and tried to take my attention away from her chest.

"Of course, you are. Where did that come from?"

"Look, I know you've been dealing with rent and everything with Lexi... I just. I don't know. Are we okay?"

"Yes, girl. I'm sorry if I've been distant lately. I do have a lot on my mind, but you are definitely still what I want."

I bit my lip and felt her fingers lift my chin up to face her and we kissed. She locked her lips onto mine and I moaned against her touch. There it was again. That spark. She hiked my leg up and clutched my thigh.

"Mmm, fuck baby. Let's go home. I feel gross still." I managed to get that out as she began kissing my neck.

She inhaled and I felt my pussy quiver. "You smell fine to me."

"No, no, I'm gross"

"Really? Let me see?"

She kissed down my belly and got down on her knees. I looked around to make sure no one was spying on us and before I knew it my pants were down and her tongue was rolling over my folds.

"Fuck C… "

I tossed my head back and she parted my lips with her tongue and made magic happen against my pores. I moaned and clutched my breast in one hand and braced myself against the car with the other. I spread my legs as far as I could with my pants around my ankle and gasped as she worked two fingers inside of me.

"Oh god… fuck… fuck."

I felt tears prick my eyes as I grew intoxicated with pleasure. The thought of someone catching a glimpse sent a thrill through my spine and I shuddered with release.

Mmm. Mmm. Mmm. I moaned and bit my lip as she lapped at my juices that dripped down my thighs. She rearranged herself to where I was bent over with my breast pressed against the car and my ass arched in her face. She dove her tongue between my cheeks and lapped at my holes.

"Oh my! Fuck! Fuck!"

The feeling of being gross and tired from work soon washed away by the waves of pleasure she released from my core.

I kicked off my pants leg and cocked my leg up against the hood of the car. She had a better grasp of my hips and latched onto my soaking pussy lips.

"Fuck. C! Fuck! Fuck! You're gonna make me cum!"

I heaved and gripped onto the hood of the car as she drove her fingers in and out of my pussy. I cried out and shook as pleasure consumed me and was released from its shackles of embarrassment.

"Baby, fuck, you're so damn good."

"Mmm, come here. Taste yourself."

I slurped my juices from her fingers and locked my lips onto hers. I sucked on her bottom lip and she moaned against me.

"Ready to go home now?"

I nodded, eager for more.

## Chapter 20

It was the middle of June when I finally heard back about one of my job applications. The company that Mrs. Valorie had pushed me to go for had accepted me as their Behavioral Health Technician. The starting pay was decent for new graduates and the workload wasn't too bad. I finished things up at the bar and collected my last check before beginning my new week at Clark County Mental Health Center. The hours were eight-hour shifts which was way more than the five I spent at the Bar. But I knew I could do it. Me and Carver had begun to grow closer and become more invested in each other's lives. I was worried that the longer hours meant I could be away from her too much but then again putting some distance between us was healthy. It would certainly be hard not seeing her every day.

I looked over myself in the mirror again before heading out. I brushed my short dark hair into a low bun and straightened the collar on my blazer. I fumbled for my bus pass in my bag and headed out the door.

It only took me a couple blocks of walking to make it to my bus on time. I grabbed a seat and sent a text to Carver letting her know I completed the first step. She was so worried about me taking the bus on my own but I kept reassuring her it was no big deal. I have to grow up at some point right?

I walked another block before I reached the building and went inside. I had a badge mailed to me and a set of keys with a fob for the door. I entered the building and found my way to the supervisors office and got myself acquainted with her. Her name was Mrs. Lucille. She made sure I received all of my materials I needed to start the job and gave me a more formal tour of the facility. Lucille was tall, had a small waist and deep red lips that shined like rubies against her brown skin. I noticed she didn't have a wedding ring on her finger, nor did she have any photos of kids around her office. I figured she must be a single woman who devoted herself to her work. When I could finally pull my eyes away from her I took a look around. When the tour was finished we talked about the important aspects of the job and what all I would be responsible for. We covered how I would run group therapy during certain times of the day and help serve meals at meal times. I got to sit and observe a couple groups and made a note of how the techs were able to keep their clients engaged and on task. It made me nervous thinking about telling a group of adults what to do and when to do it but part of me felt like I could ease into the role.

"So what do you think about the job?"

I took a sip of my green tea and thought for a moment before I answered Lucille. "I think it will be a good learning opportunity. A great place to grow."

She smiled and sipped her coffee. "Val was right about you. I do see a lot of potential in you girl."

I blushed and finished my tomato sandwhich.

"If you ever need anything… " She let her eyes gloss over me and smiled. "My door is always open."

I nodded and grabbed my things up to head home for the day.

"This may be out of place but I was just curious about something… were you and Valorie close?"

I hesitated and sat back down. What was she getting at? I obviously can't tell her how I fucked my last employer.

Especially not on my first day.

"Um, well yeah professionally speaking."

I tucked a strand of phantom hair behind my ear and clutched onto the pile of empty wrappers and plates.

"Interesting. Well… " She slid her hand over and placed it on top of mine and I looked up and met her eye to eye. "Well, I hope that we also can be close."

I took a hard swallow, wishing I still had something to put in my mouth to keep me from having to talk. "Oh yes, ma'am. Of course."

"Good girl."

There's that fucking phrase I adore. I felt a tingle shoot through my body. I felt the need to let her know I only meant in the work-related sense.

"Professionally."

"Mhm. Of course. It was nice to meet you, Azlyn."

She slid her hand away from mine and I felt as if I was holding my breath. I took a deep breath and sighed. She sashayed back to her office, and I gathered my things to head home. I suddenly really missed Carver.

***

When I made it back home it was close to 7pm and growing dark out. I walked up to the door and let myself in. There was music playing and I heard Carver giggling. When I walked into the living room she was with none other than Lexi. Lexi was dancing and Carver was sitting on the couch with a beer. I didn't know they were on speaking let alone visiting times again. I dropped my bag and went over to the couch to stand behind Carver. I noticed her bite her lip and her eyes never left Lexi. Lexi saw me and stopped dancing and folded her arms across her chest.

"Oh, hey babe, you scared me."

"I didn't want to interrupt."

I put my arms on either side of her and braced myself on the back of the couch and looked down at her.

"There's nothing to interrupt."

She smiled up at me and I could smell the alcohol on her breath. She had more than one bottle of beer. "I missed you."

"I don't know, you look pretty entertained to me?" I tried to hide the jealousy in my voice, but it dripped through anyways.

"Are you jealous?"

She giggled and tilted her head back to take another swig of the bottle. I swiped it from her and swallowed her swig finishing the bottle.

"Of what?"

"Huh, well I guess I should go." Lexi dramatically sighed and stormed off towards the door.

Carver stood to go after her, but I stopped her.

"Don't. You've been drinking too much."

"What? I'm fine."

Carver went after Lexi and I heard them whispering and giggling at the door. I walked up to them and watched Carver let her out the door.

"I don't want that to happen again."

"What to happen?"

"All the giggling and whispering and her dirty dancing for you!"

I felt tears prick my eyes as my heart swelled with envy and anger.

"What are you talking about? You don't have a re—reason to be—be jealoush."

"You've been drinking too much." My voice was quieter now.

She ran her fingers through her hair and squished her eyes closed and opened them again. She was probably starting to feel the weight of the alcohol in her system.

"Carver… "

She looked at me as if she was about to cry and I knew she had definitely drunk too much. I'd never seen her cry before. I rushed over to her and let my lips apologize for me. I didn't want to fight. Not with her. And not right now. She kissed me back and giggled against me. Suddenly her giggles no longer irritated me.

"I want you, C."

"I want you, Azzie."

Hearing her slur my name sent chills down my spine. We made our way to the bed, and I straddled myself on top of her. I kissed her breast and made my way down her tummy. She spread her legs and allowed me access to devour her. I stroked her clit with my tongue in small circles and slid my tongue along her slickened slit. I wondered what exactly it was that made her moist. Her dancing or my kiss. I shoved the thought away and sighed against her. She whimpered and twitched her legs at my touch. I blew gently against her lips and parted them with my fingers. I kissed her and lapped at her hole. I let my tongue fondle its way into her hole and licked around in circles tasting the juices dripping from her walls.

"Ooo, fuck baby."

Her hips began to buck against my touch, and she moved her pussy up and down with my tongue dancing inside of her.

"Damn, baby fuck me. Oh my god."

She bucked faster and I took my fingers and rubbed her clit side to side. She gripped my head pressing me deeper into her. I stretched my tongue as far as it could go and let her have her way with my face deep in her pussy.

"Oh my god, oh my god, fuck, fuck yes, yes."

She clenched her thighs together over my head and bucked against me for a final time before releasing me and letting her body go limp as she took in deep breaths.

Juices began spilling out of her hole and I slurped them up.

"Damn girl."

She pulled me on top of her and began licking my chin and up to my lips. She kissed me and I kissed her back allowing her to taste herself off me.

"You're so fucking good at that."

"I like you, Carver."

She kissed me and wrapped me in her arms. She let her arms trace down my back and grab my ass and tug at my hips. I moaned as my clit slid against her flesh and her lips fell to my neck biting and kissing my flesh.

"God! Fuck!"

I pressed myself deeper into her, impressed with hot wet I already was. I gripped the sheets beside her and let my lips meet hers in a deep embrace. Another couple of fucks later and I was cumming and trembling against her.

"Kiss me, baby."

I kissed her and we held each other until we fell asleep.

When I opened my eyes again, I was in a hospital room. Panic crept in. My parents were sitting across from me sitting in a sofa. I was hooked up to IV's and a nurse had walked in.

"Where... Where am I?"

"Oh honey!"

My parents woke up and embraced me. I stood rigid still, still in shock. I had no idea how I got here and where I was.

"Oh, good you're awake."

She smiled at me and checked my IV's.

"You were in a wreck, sweetie."

I looked at the nurse trying to make sense of everything.

"But... but... where's Carver?"

"Was that the young lady you were in the car with?" my dad asked and looked at the Nurse when I didn't speak.

"No... here it says the other girl was a Rebecca Hall. Your classmate."

My heart thudded in my ears drowning out the voices around me.

"How... " My voice was hoarse, and I was fighting back tears. "How long have I been here?"

"It's been about a week hun. The doctor just wanted to monitor you. If you're curious about the day it's May 3$^{rd}$."

That's the week right before graduation. I began shaking. This wasn't real. This couldn't be happening. None of this made any sense. I was just in bed with Carver. I had just graduated. I was starting a new life...

"No, no this isn't right. Something's wrong."

"I can get the doctor if I need to, ma'am."

"No, no this isn't right! This isn't right! I'm not supposed to be here. I was with Carver! We... we! Fuck. No!"

My parents were holding me down and the nurse had left to go get the doctor. I looked towards the door just before it closed, and I saw a glimpse of Rebecca standing across the hall looking at me. Her face was pale, and she was staring dead at me. I shook my head and felt a chill shoot through me.

"No... No... "

I shook my head as reality crept in and the memories of a time spent with Carver began slipping away as if it was some long dream that needed to be wiped from my memory once I woke up. I grasped at the sheets and stopped resisting when the last shred vanished from my mind.

I stood still staring at Rebecca and she stared back at me.